I0699261

Awry

Stories

A number of stories in this collection have been revised for this edition. The following have been previously published: "Father's Work" in *North American Review*; "Mother, I Have Dreamed of You" in *Juked*; "As Wide, as Deep: a heart and a hole" in *Wordriot*; "In the Swamp between the Cities and Shore, a Girl" in *Tinge*; "After the Ossuary" in *COG*; "Nonconcentric" in *Matter Press*; "The Light for Both of Us" in *Banango Street*; "Phone Etiquette" in *The Denver Quarterly*; and "The Fine Set of Teeth" in *Meat for Tea*.

Published by Bridge Eight Press
Jacksonville, Florida

www.bridgeeight.com

ISBN 9798218591052
LCCN 2025931109

Printed in the USA
Book design by Caleb Michael Sarvis
Cover by duncan b. barlow

For Alisa

Stories

Awry

Stories

[T]he sadness, mourning, and melancholy (Traurigkeit) of nature and of animality are born out of this muteness (Stummheit, Sprachlosigkeit), but also out of and by means of the wound without a name: that of having been given a name. Finding oneself deprived of language, one loses the power to name, to name oneself, indeed to respond to one's name. (As if man didn't also receive his name and his names!)

Jacques Derrida on Walter Benjamin's
"On Language as Such and on the Language of Man"

Part I

Phone Etiquette

I don't know why he started doing it. Calling after he killed my child. It started a few months after a farmer discovered her body in an irrigation ditch just south of town. My brother had convinced me to collect Kimberly's belongings and store them in his basement to assuage my grief. I had just returned, my arms feeling the phantom pains of my deceased child's belongings, as if they shouldn't have come away from them so freely.

As I opened the door, I was greeted by the ringing rotary phone my husband had purchased days prior to leaving us with a note declaring his unbearable sadness under what he called "the oppressive foot of domesticity." When he left, I'd wanted to break the phone, but Kimberly loved the chime of its bell and convinced me to keep it on the kitchen wall. She'd sit on the floor waiting patiently for her father to ring. When she gave up waiting, I didn't have the heart to replace it. With this memory in my head, I rushed to the kitchen and grabbed the yellow plastic handset; perhaps her father had heard the news; perhaps he wanted to come back and make amends. I would've liked to think I'd tell him he could never come back but know now I would have let him return. It's what she would have wanted, after all.

My heartbeat rattled in my neck as I pulled the receiver to my ear. I remember how cold it was. Hard. There was silence, or a kind of silence. The crackling silence that fills a telephone wire. When I lowered the phone, I heard someone clear his throat. I spoke again. They took a deep breath and then the line went dead. I was convinced it was my husband. It was just the thing he would do. Attempt the right thing but stop short of it.

It wasn't for another few weeks that it happened again. The seasons had just changed and the extended family had come over with a spring dinner. The air was crisp and smelled of onion grass, so I left the door open to the screen. Though it was dusk, a few children lingered in the yards playing tag. Their voices were so jovial. My womb was suddenly aware of its emptiness. Part of me wanted to close the door, but a larger part of me wanted to hear the children laugh. It seemed to be the only feeling I'd had in months. Memories of Kimberly emerged and it seemed as if the world around me had dissolved completely, the outside voices acting as the soundtrack to my waking dream. From that came the sound of the phone. At first, a part of the memory and finally drawing me from it. I answered and was once again greeted by starchy silence. Eager to return to the sound of children, I hung up. It was only a few seconds later that it rang again. This time, I hadn't even said hello before a man whispered, I miss Kimberley.

The officials were unable to trace the call. They were convinced that it was my husband. I told them I was unsure. There was a time when I thought I'd never forget the timbre of his voice, but I realized then how easily a voice could be forgotten. That night I couldn't sleep. The words repeated themselves inside me. Why would someone do this to me? If it was my husband, was he aware of our daughter's murder? Was he so cruel as to call and hang up like that? Certainly, he was cruel enough to leave Kimberly and me, but to do this?

Giving up the attempt to find rest, I resolved myself to removing the phone he'd purchased. The yellow plastic machine came away from the wall much easier than I had expected. I disconnected the coil line and placed the cradle, handset, and cord into an old box. When I dropped it into the garbage outside, it gave a muffled ding I found oddly haunting at the time. Perhaps I still do.

The salesman at the phone store told me that it was a shame I needed a phone so soon because he'd heard rumors a phone with a push button dial pad was soon to be released. This, he assured me, would revolutionize the way people interacted with phones. Although I was admittedly put off by his unnecessary conversation in regard to future phones, he did assist me in purchasing a fine brown phone. Upon my return, I placed it on the wall and was convinced then the new phone would make a change in my life (the bad spell of my husband's phone having been exorcised from the home). Testing the phone, I called my sister-in-law. The call was successful.

When a mother loses a child, she never wants to forget the sound of her baby's voice, the smell of her hair, the touch of her hand. This much, I understood; however, what had never occurred to me were the intangible things. The house, for example, felt hopelessly lifeless. I began to resent it. I wanted to feel at home, but never could. I started to leave the radio on so I could come home to something besides the haunting silence.

My brother attempted to alleviate my feelings of loneliness by bringing me a dog. Although his thoughts were well intentioned, I couldn't separate the intention from the idea he was trying to replace Kimberly with an animal. At first, I agreed to take the dog, as it was a rescue and I did, admittedly now, feel bad for the beast, but, as the demands of the thing grew, so did my intolerance for it.

Through my sleepless nights, the dog would curl into a warm crescent and carry on with fitful, dream-filled, naps. Its legs occasionally quivering. Its mouth emitting yips and sighs. It wasn't long before I came to dislike it. For many reasons. As my insomnia mounted, it found sleep easily. It attempted most nights to crawl atop my bed, putting first a paw, then its nose, and finally making sad eyes at me. This, I could not abide by; after all, Kimberly, once her father abandoned us, slept by my side; what would she think of me trying to replace her with a dog in the bed? After a few nights of this, I began to question why this dog's life had been spared, but Kimberly's wasn't. Why did people seek to save dogs and allow children to die alone in ditches? No, the dog didn't comfort me.

The next call came the night my boss imposed upon me an involuntary medical leave. I assured him I could perform my duties, but he insisted that my work had become "rough around the edges," "sometimes illegible," and that I'd grown "unsightly." I'd just heated a meal my sister-in-law had provided me, a luxury she afforded on account of what she called my "lingering trauma," when the phone rang. It was with great hesitation I put my hand on the receiver; something warned me not to answer. However, in the event it was my sister-in-law, I didn't want to be perceived as ungrateful for her help. Placing the handset against my ear, I heard a man breathing. He had a cold. I could almost feel the nasal congestion through the line. Who is this, I asked. I miss Kimberley, he replied and the line fell dead.

My body gave. There was nothing left in me. I must have hit my head on the counter because I came to on the floor with the dog licking my face. The lights were beautiful then, kaleidoscoping around its shaggy head. It was such a thing of wonder that I allowed the dog to continue, and, for a moment, I felt some empathy towards the damned thing. As I found equilibrium with reality, I became acutely aware of the clicking phone line. I attempted to recall the voice but found myself thinking of my husband. Why would he call me? What terrible thing had I done to provoke this?

Placing a bag of frozen peas on the crown of my skull, I retreated into the sunroom, which once served as my husband's office, and made use of his stationery to ink a list of things I had done in my life that might have brought this upon me. It stood to reason just then, that Kimberley was innocent, pure, that no one would have wanted to harm her. It also stood to reason that the calls were not intended to disrespect my murdered child, but to wound me again. I eliminated any women. My final list contained: the man I left for my husband, the father of three who couldn't pay his mortgage (and who I subsequently had to sign foreclosure papers on), and my husband, as he found life with Kimberley and me unbearable. Below each name, I placed a category of unlikely, likely, and very likely.

My brother said I was being irrational. He attributed my idea to my lack of sleep, my head trauma, my loss. He and his wife asked me to see a doctor. Reluctantly, I agreed. I stayed at their place that evening but could not sleep. They had a large collection of fashion magazines, so I flipped through them until dawn. When I heard my brother's alarm, I turned off the light and feigned sleep. It was not my habit to be dishonest, but my lack of sleep began to bother those closest to me. It was not but a year ago that Kimberly had asked me if it was ever okay to lie. I told her it wasn't. As I sat at the breakfast table that morning and lied about my good night of sleep, I wondered if she was frowning at me from heaven. This thought nearly brought me to tears, a reaction that was not lost on my sister-in-law. When she asked if I was okay, I told another white lie. This made me feel worse.

Three weeks into my therapy sessions, which had increased to twice a week, I got another call. He, my husband or his imposter, began to call once a week after that. When I spoke to my therapist, I did not mention the calls. He occasionally asked if I had received any more and I lied. Frequently, I would burst into tears after lying, but as the lies increased, so did my tolerance. As if each lie coated me a little more. This, it occurred to me, was how someone gained a hard outer shell. She commits enough transgressions it's impossible for anyone to get to the meat of her. There was something comforting about it, and if I'm to be honest here, some days it felt like this new exoskeleton was the only thing left.

To be fair, it's easy to fool a therapist. He can only go by what you give him, and I gave him the tasty pieces he wanted, things to analyze but never the things I wanted to keep to myself. I'd tell him I was sad about my daughter, which was true, but I framed it in a way that made it look like I was making positive changes in my life. I said, for example, that I had just taken up a new exercise regimen. This couldn't have been further from the truth. Most days I barely made it out of my bed. I'd sit there and stare at the dog, for which I was oddly beginning to develop affection for. This newfound connection began on one of the nights I was able to find an hour of sleep. I had a dream where I was sitting in the back yard. The sun was warm but soft. The dog was playing fetch with someone. The sound was strange in that way it is in dreams, like it's in a cave or underwater. Echoing and muffled at once. From this chaos came Kimberly's laugh. I sat up to find her hugging the dog. Kissing his square skull. Mommy, she said, finally, you got me a doggie. They ran toward me. Tackled me. We laughed.

When I awoke, I was spooning the dog. So it was, I began to associate him with Kimberly. But not in the way I had feared Kimberly would think. After all, I reminded myself, one could never replace a person with a dog. Kimberly had, in fact, reached out to me in my dream to let me know. This truth, which seemed self-evident to me, was lost on my therapist who told me the dream was my subconscious making sense of my grief and helping me heal and forgive myself for my daughter's death. It was on that day that I felt much better for having lied to my therapist, as he was a purveyor of misinformation.

Why, I wondered, was everyone trying to get me to forget my lovely daughter? Why was it so important for me to move forward, to live without her as if she'd never been born? Could they not understand the pain of my loss?

I began to skip my therapy sessions, first calling in with excuses and finally forgoing the calls altogether. For a few weeks, he called to check in on me, but soon got the hint and abandoned his pursuit of what he called my "mental wellbeing." He did, however, call my brother and express his concern.

It was a warm summer afternoon when my brother came by after work to check up on me. I didn't open the door for him but watched him from my bedroom window instead. This would have been the end to his intrusion, except I'd forgotten he had a key to the house, and so, he let himself inside. Had I expected him to commit such an unspeakable intrusion on my privacy, I might have changed the locks or at the very least, cleaned the house; however, this was not the case. He made his way to my bedroom, where he found me bundled in my covers, the dog resting its head on my thighs.

I feigned sleep, but he was not fooled. I'm worried about you, sis, he said. We are worried about you. I assured him there was nothing to worry about. I was grieving but finding peace. He pointed out that my home was very unkempt and that there was food "in decay" on the kitchen counters, in the trash, and some on the floor. I allowed him this but said I'd been busy lately and I had, in fact, planned on cleaning that very evening. He saw through this and said he'd be happy to help me clean, that he and his wife would come by after dinner and do it for me. When I declined, he made a face. A frown perhaps or something quite like it. Then, as if on cue, he told me I needed to continue my sessions, that my home reflected my mental state. Again, I feigned sleep, but once again my brother was not fooled.

After my brother left, I decided I should take the dog for a walk. We wandered the streets for several hours before he eventually led me to the very sight where my sweet Kimberly had been murdered. This I took as a sign from Kimberly. That she wanted me to meditate on her murder. The dog and I perched on the edge of the irrigation ditch where the insects winked in the still water. Mosquitos stabbed at my flesh. A few at first, but soon my skin began to burn. Still, we did not move. I spoke to the dog about Kimberly, about her murder, about my dream. The dog leaned into me, placed its head on my lap, and fell to sleep. I stroked one of his soft floppy ears and allowed the bugs to feast on me. Around the time dusk began took the sky, I found myself compelled to wade into the water. It was warm and viscous. I dipped into it, lay back and tried to float for a moment. Then, I tried to sink. It was no easy deed, but I managed, and just as I was about to open my mouth and allow the silty water to fill my lungs, The dog breached the surface and tugged at the cuff of my pants. At first, I thought he was trying to help me descend to the bottom, but soon realized he was trying to pull me back toward the bank. I took this as a sign from Kimberly and found my way out of the water.

It didn't take long for the infection to set in, a day or two at best. The small bites I had scratched into pockets and further still until they lay open and bleeding like angry mouths, had filled with the infection and my blood went septic. My fever began to alter my vision, my voice, my thoughts. It must have been the latter that drove me to stumble into the kitchen and phone my brother. I don't, of course, remember this and often wonder if he once again invaded my home, perhaps to make good on his threats to clean. I awoke in a hospital bed, my brother's wife needling away at an afghan.

She said they were glad "I called" and they took it as a "good sign" I had. She spoke loudly and slowly as if I'd gone deaf. We, she began, think you may be healing. I wondered how that opinion would have changed if I'd told them that, not only did I procure my infection by returning to the scene of my daughter's death and try to drown myself, but that I was in a fever induced delusion when I'd called them and didn't remember doing it. Furthermore, how would she react if I had acted on my impulse at that particular moment and accused them of once more entering my home illegally and finding me asleep? Instead, I did what I had recently grown so deft at, I lied.

It was during my time in the hospital I began to grow very anxious. I was missing something; I was sure of it. My brother assured me he was looking after the dog and my house. He said he even mowed the lawn and trimmed the bushes. This, I told him, was appreciated, but these were not the things from which my anxiety arose. Rather, it was something else. Perhaps, I said when dozing off to sleep, I missed the comfort of the dog. And it was in this thought I found myself in a waking dream or a dreaming state of wakefulness, and I saw Kimberly and the dog resting beneath a small oak tree in the corner of my hospital room. When I stepped across the room, the way one steps in a dream, working with little advancement, they grew more distant and my heart buckled beneath the weight of my disappointment. As the life seemed to seep from me and the world began to melt, I awoke to a nurse telling me I was due to be discharged and that I should be happy to return home. I'm not sure why, but my hands grasped the rails of my hospital bed. The nurse asked if I was in pain and I said I was. This, I assured myself, was true, but my body was beyond pain and deep down, past the words of comfort, I knew this. She gave me a small white pill and my eyes went dark with a long dreamless sleep.

When I was released and returned to my home, things were different. First, the house had been cleaned. From the floors to the counter; from the walls to the appliances; even the sheets had been replaced. They had painted my living room a lighter color, removed the thick curtains that blocked the sun, washed the windows. My sister-in-law put potted plants, trees, and hanging air plants in every room. She said the foliage would purify the air and cleanse my spirit. My brother, when he welcomed me home, told me they were so proud of my ability to overcome my loss they wanted to do something special for me. He walked me upstairs and revealed that they had converted Kimberly's bedroom into a gym.

I bit my lip in a fake and painful smile; it was all I could do to keep from collapsing. This room conversion, I assured myself, in the way one does when she thinks she may collapse, was a result of my lies, those tiny white lies that gave me my exoskeleton, and because of this, I had to take it in stride. It was evident to me I would never touch the expensive equipment they bought; I would return to the room when they left and attempt to cry, but as they stood there, their faces on fire with the satisfaction of their good deed, I could only thank them and tell them that I was lucky to have them in my life. This was, from a purely objective point of view, true; however, it was in my own way, just another tiny lie, which, I thought at that moment, may betray me later in my life.

The days after my return were a gluttonous mass of hours I scarcely remember outside of feeding the dog scraps of the food they'd left for me. We had taken to sleeping in the back yard. I carried some covers and pillows from the bedroom and lay them beneath the shade of a few magnolia trees in the corner. Kimberly used to love the magnolia trees for their thick climbing branches and fragrant blooms in the spring. Once a day, she would carry a bloom from one of the trees and place it in a bowl of water, its petals splayed wide like some fantastic water creature; she would watch it float and beg me to come and sniff it. Look it! she'd say, Look it! I brought you a flower; it smells like clean sheets and stars and springtime. It is only now that I realize how right she was. The blooms smelled like all of those things. It worked my heart at the time, watching all those flowery things die in a bowl of water, but I grew to forget about them and only saw the love of my Kimberly, her sense of wonder not quite Earth-bound yet.

It was one night, when the air was warm and the scent of the magnolia leaves was nearly palpable when the phone rang again.

At first, it was lost in the soft clamor of the leaves in a breeze, but soon, it birthed itself more clearly and I ran into the house. As my hand touched the phone, it stopped. I stood there for some time. I'm not sure how long. It could have been minutes, but it felt to me like hours. My heart was heavy with its own tissue. Eventually, it came to life again with another call. I snatched the receiver and pulled it to my ear. I miss Kimberly, he said. Before he was able to hang up, I replied, I miss Kimberly too. There was a sound of air catching in lungs and then the familiar click of a dead line.

The following afternoon, I left the house again and returned to the phone store where I was greeted by the same enthusiastic young salesman. I asked him for one hundred feet of cable for my phone. His face twisted in a strange pucker. He held his finger up in the air as if he aimed to touch something and turned toward the back room. There, I saw him interact with an older man, a manager perhaps, bald at the top with a soft fringe of hair along the sides of his scalp. They submerged themselves farther into the gloom and reemerged with several packages of wire and a few connector boxes. As the young man placed the packages into a bag, the older gentleman came from the back with a brown phone which had twelve square buttons on its face.

The younger man burst into a delighted smile and said, Ma'am, this is the new style of phone I told you about the last time you were here. With the hands of a model, he touched the phone, lifted the hand set from the cradle, fondled the buttons as if undressing it. This will change the world, he said. Imagine transmitting ideas through this. Communicating with databanks. Making selections on menus. It's all possible in the future.

To indulge him, I pressed a couple buttons. I had to admit it was nice not having to roll the dialer, and had it not been for the fact that there was no one for me to call outside of my brother and his wife, I may have purchased the revolutionary phone. Instead, I bought the items they had previously bagged for me and made my way home where I extended the phone cord through the house, across the yard, and around the bole of the largest tree, where I had hammered a nail and hung the phone. I then curled my body on the blankets and watched the small points of light filter through the leaves, bright like stars, white like clean laundry, and warm like spring. I scratched at the bandages the hospital had put over my infected wounds, and when that wasn't helping, I removed them and scratched at the scabs. Some came away, opening their red mouths to my fingers, others remained and only came free after multiple attempts to satisfy my itch.

On the day I first saw Kimberly in the yard, she was faint, as if painted into the air with pale watercolors. It was only an instant. She was stooped over, calling the dog to her. The dog stood from his spot and walked. Before he got to her, he lay in the sun and turned to expose the shag of his underbelly. Playing hard to get, I thought. I tried to sit up so she could better see me, but she was gone before I was able to manage it. The heat of jealousy flushed my cheeks as I watched the dog roll back and forth along the ridge of his spine. Why, after all, would she have called out to the dog and not her own mother? It was not long before I found my reason again. A mother should not seek to impose joy onto her child but should celebrate the things in which her child finds joy. The following day, Kimberly visited again, this time sitting upon the crook of a branch overhead. She smiled at me. I love you, I said. She didn't reply. She waved and faded soon after. On the third day she appeared, it was near dusk and she was wrapped in the blankets beside me. She looked to the open wounds on my arms and legs, the small insects that flew and crawled around them, and she frowned. Lifting my hand to touch the hair loping from behind her ear, I fell over toward her, and with that, she was gone.

The phone rang while I was sleeping. I had been dreaming of a river thick with mud, the dog on the banks tearing at his stomach with bleeding fangs, me somewhere in the thick of the current. I answered, and, without thinking, said, I've seen her. However, it was not the mystery caller; it was my brother, who asked me who I'd seen, and why I hadn't answered the door when he'd come over. We had an agreement I wouldn't enter without permission, he said, but that you'd keep in touch so that I wouldn't have to. I told him that I'd been busy. That I'd been hiking with the dog and spending long hours in the outdoors. From there I began to tell him how majestic the park was in the morning and that there was a delightful hiking trail not ten minutes from the neighborhood that went for miles. None of this being true, I stumbled a bit when he asked if he and his wife could join us for a hike over the weekend. I wish, I replied, but I promised my boss that I would spend the weekend catching up on some of the work I missed during my leave of absence. My brother told me we should celebrate, that he and my sister-in-law recently had purchased a few bottles of wine from a local winery and they were looking for just such an occasion to uncork one. I mentioned I couldn't drink on my antibiotics, but that I would love to join them sometime in the following week. This, I thought at that time, would give me time to find a reason to back out. Before he hung up, he asked who I had seen again. Janet, my new partner at work, I said. I'd just gotten off the phone with my boss and forgot to tell him I'd met with her. I thought he was calling back. Lying had become second nature to me by then.

In many ways, it soothed me, much the way knitting soothes my sister-in-law.

I spent the next few hours thinking of new stories I could tell my brother to defer his visitation. I would have to call him, perhaps every day, as a means to circumvent his intrusion. It seemed to me a good way to pass the hours as I waited; waiting for what I couldn't say. Then the phone rang. I answered again, this time hesitating for the other to speak first. I miss Kimberly, he said. I see her, I said, I see her in the yard. He breathed on the other line, heavy and rhythmic. He hung up and my body fall limp. The following morning I called my brother. It made him happy I'd called, he said. It was another sign of my progression. My wellness. Of course, I said, my voice slightly thickened by the phlegm that had begun to nest in my throat. I'm as a healthy as a peach. When finished with the call, I felt for the first time, what I have come to accept as a fever. It began as body warmth I attributed to, first the blankets, then the sun, and finally the infection that had developed or redeveloped in my body. As the day progressed, the fever controlled me. I shook and sweat, my head pounding savagely. There was little I remembered, just long bouts of sleep where I awoke too weak to stand. I remember Kimberly sitting by me for a few moments. At one point, I thought I saw her trying to clean me after I'd soiled the sheets. I say, thought, as I seem to recall feeling her presence more than seeing her. Nonetheless, her presence was certainly real to me then, and to a lesser degree now, as I take a moment to recall it.

It was from one of these bouts of sleep I remember waking up with the phone in my hand. I was talking but to whom I can't quite recall. My throat had closed in upon itself and felt as if a funnel spider had crawled inside me and crafted a most fantastic web. Even as I remember it now, I remember the vision I had in my head of the drab little arachnid, snug in its funnel of silk. I repeated, as best I could, in what I must now admit was most likely a very unintelligible language, that I missed Kimberly. And then the world went black.

When I awoke, I was in a small hospital room. There were nurses with masks and gowns and loose-fitting caps upon their heads. At first, I thought I'd seen an orb of light glowing between them, a pulsating sphere of pure energy, which, at that moment, as I can best recall, was the source of all life, the energy which Kimberly had returned to and which was calling me to join my beautiful daughter. And from that glow, I saw a small hand reach for me and I, in return, attempted to reach for it. As my hand lifted from the bed, one of the nurses pushed it back. No, I said, she wants me to come to her. Then, as if on cue, the light began to fade and I saw that it was not the hand of my daughter, but the hand of another nurse who was approaching with a syringe and that the orb of light was no more than sunlight. Poor thing, you've been through so much, the nurse cooed. You'll be better soon. As the medication eased into me, the world began to grow soft around the edges. How could I ever feel better, I wondered. How could I ever feel whole again?

I wasn't awake much for the next few days. I remember a doctor appearing in what I thought was a dream. He, just a ghostly figure between the narrowed slits of my eyes, spoke to me about the procedure I was to undergo to save what they could. Of what, I remember wondering as his voice began to fade and my eyes shut. There were a few other times I woke up after that. Once to find Kimberly petting the dog in the doorway. When I called her name, she smiled and took the dog into the hallway and walked from view. The second time I awoke, I saw my sister-in-law praying with a rosary, her brow knotted with worry. I tried to speak her name but was too weak.

It was the pain in my legs that woke me again. I attempted to sit up and touch them, but found my body unwilling to move in the way to which I was accustomed. Searching the room to find no one there, I called for help to no avail. I found a small cable dangling from the bedrail. Pulling it into my palm, I grasped it tightly and depressed the red button until a nurse came to me. She smiled and said it was good to see me awake. She then told me that my brother was downstairs buying some lunch and would be up any moment. My legs, I said, feel as if there is a great weight upon them. Did she have a pill to take the pain away? It was a strange frown she gave me at first and then she said that I should wait until my brother returned before they did anything with my legs. She retreated into the hall-way and I continued my attempts to sit up, failing with each effort. This, of course, did not deter me because I felt lucid for the first time in what seemed like many days; how many, I was still unsure. It was during one of my attempts to sit up, locking my hands around the bedrails and gritting my teeth against the weakness in my back, which also became painful as I struggled, my brother spoke at the door. Please, Sis, he said, you're too weak to sit up yet. You've not eaten solid food in over a week. I released my grip, allowed my body to go limp, sighed. My legs hurt, I said. Is there something on them? Oh Sis, he said, his voice soft much the way it was when he'd heard the news of Kimberly's murder.

They moved me into my brother's house where I would remain, they said, until I was able to function on my own. They said that I was "unable to function as an able-bodied individual" and that I had many months of physical therapy and trauma therapy to help me transition back into my old life. It was in this therapy where I was given the task to think these past few months through. To come to some kind of understanding as to why I was unable to process the loss of my daughter in a healthy way. It is difficult for me, even now, to understand what they meant by healthy. Yet, to appease them, I write a journal. The phone doesn't ring and I only see Kimberly when I'm asleep. I long to return home. To speak to the only person who seems to miss Kimberly as much as I do. Until I can return, I will attend therapy and pretend that my child never existed. That this was all some terrible dream.

Of Flesh and Fur

Though the house felt empty, I did not crave the council of coyotes. I shut my curtains to them. Ensured my cans were huddled inside the garage. Left no scrap or drink to lure them to me. Still they came. Sniffing and yipping along the house. Their paws often tip-tapping on the doors and windows.

They'd come from the hills. Forced by sprawl. There were murmurs of conspiracy. Something about a university experiment gone awry. Though it remained unconfirmed, the news reported sightings of a toddler among their ranks. The anchors laughed. Said they better call child services. That some people had too much time on their hands. Then said it takes all kinds, doesn't it? It seemed to me they actually didn't know all the kinds of people it took. That was the trade off when living in a small town. Safety in exchange for naivety. There'd been, after all, documented cases of people raised by wild dogs. Wolves. Feral cats. Even the legend of Pecos Bill. But how possible would it be? To survive a year. To endure the unforgiving winter. A feeling came then. Something working at my finger. A ghostly mouth.

I locked the doors. Bolted the security bars. Closed the garage. I lay on my couch and thought of how I used to feed the animals. The birds. The squirrels. The coyotes. Then. Then I thought of the boy running wild with the pack. Sniffing at my windows. Looking for me.

II.

It was a time when science made all things possible. We were drawing shapes in the air with 3D pens. Curing diseases with bits of babies. Digging trains under seas. We were a new age. An age of correcting the wrongs of previous years. Perfecting our bodies. Improving our lives.

It was a time when our bodies could defy age. Almost. Almost, because age changes us. We weep at commercials. Needle our palms. Grind our teeth. Wave to children. And so it was that I was childless. No wife to chamber a life. The family line falling to ashes with my death. It was no matter to me when I was young. Too busy travelling. Spending my money. Buying a house full of things. Screens and wood and fabric.

My desire to have a child began when I was organizing my basement. Transferring musty things from weary cardboard boxes to sleek plastic containers. It was a thing of beauty. All clear and labeled. Light upon them in clean, straight lines. In that wrack of cardboard, I discovered a picture of my father and I. A photo of him bouncing me on his knee. Had I not seen this before? And, if I had, why couldn't I remember it?

I thought for a time—my mind unable to recapture what it perhaps knew. Until. Until I returned to the work. From there, each relic took on a new definition. A box of rare treasures, archived. A photo, a jewel. A paper clipping, a sacred object. First, I placed them all in separate binders. Plastic covers to protect them. Hand numbered and accounted for. Where would these things go? This house of woods, glasses, and metals? The photos of my father. His stories and those he carried from the past forward. Would all whispers be sucked away?

I lay in bed that night and it prodded me. A bird pecking at my chest. *Let me out.* When I fell to sleep, I dreamed of a brown river fed by a vast white ocean. I floated there, the current leading me to land. A surge of water crested the tree line, and when I passed the conflux, the wave towered behind me. Collapsed onto me. And in the tumble, I heard a solitary word. *Baby.*

*

The next day, while reconciling accounts for a client, I couldn't shake the word from my head. *Baby,* I typed in a column for *Barbeque.* *Child,* I typed instead of *Chili.* I needed to clear my head. Take a lunch break. I drove past the artificial reproductive facility. Thought on it. U-turned.

I spoke to a woman for some time. I made it clear that I was interested in donating my semen for someone to use. For a baby to be birthed and continue my family line. It was when I said to her that I wanted to pass forward the stories, that she said, No. No, I asked. No, she said again. My DNA was to be forfeited.

Sterilized of unique labeling markers and re-encoded with the new family's name. They needed only my seed. All genetic flaws and familial markers would be stripped. It struck me as funny. How far we'd come and yet there was some mystery to conception that science couldn't quite decode. They still needed biological donations.

She then handed me a card of a colleague. An expert in the field of identical genetic reproduction. A clone, I asked. Yes, she said.

I didn't like the idea. In fact, I almost didn't accept the card. But, I did. Then. Then I tossed it in the trash at home.

That bird again pecked. I chewed at my lip. Popped my anxious ankles. Thought of my father's stories of fights in college. Of his victories in football. Of him teaching me how to throw a punch. Of the word *breadbasket* as a part of his concept of human anatomy. I fingered my sternum. Dipped my fingertip below the bone. Pressed.

The next day I met with the scientist. Still undecided. About to leave. To drive home. But she offered me a coffee and a Danish. That's really what it boiled down to. I stayed because I wanted the Danish. We sat in her office and she told me about the process of cloning, about the perks and of the hazards. For example, the child would come to me as an infant, but he'd have developed in an extrauterine fetal incubator. She mentioned then a few of the clones were perceived as *cold* for not having known connection to a mother. She then spoke to me about telomeres. About the percentage of clones that expire early. About percentages of anomalies. About genetic flaws from the donor continuing on inside the boy. Yes, yes, I assured her. Eating the Danish and then asking for another.

*

In the months I waited for my child, I busied myself by prepping the house. Putting foam on sharp corners. Hammering nails that had wiggled loose in the floorboards. Adding locks on the cabinets. Then. Then I moved all of my ex-wife's things from the sewing room. Built a crib. Painted the walls. Clouds, animals, stars. I tried to remember what I had liked as a boy. What my parents had done for me. I thought of them painting my walls. Of my father building my crib. What hopes they must have had before it all went to shit. Before the drink and the fights and the divorce and the death. It occurred to me then, sitting on the floor, I had a chance to get this right.

When my ex-wife came to retrieve her dusty sewing machine, I was outside filling my squirrel feeder. Loading a hardened cob of corn onto a small table. It was a thing of beauty to watch the squirrels sit on the little chair. Feast at the table like gentlemen. She looked at me. You're still feeding them? she asked. Yes, I said. And the coyotes, did you start feeding them again? Yes, I said.

She shook her head and asked if she might look around the house and see if she'd left anything else. All those years ago. When she went to work but never came home. Found a new home. Another man. A manly man, my friends called him. A cop. A man who built furniture that didn't come from a box. Gave her two baby boys and a girl. Before her womb went sour.

I loaded her machine into the back of the car. Looked at the smashed animal crackers on the floor. The baby seat cushions stained with various drinks. A curly straw wedged between seats. My ex-wife walked outside. What is that, she asked. What is what, I asked. The room, she said. I'm having a baby, I said. Now, she asked. Yes, I said. She called me an asshole. Slapped me. Why didn't you want a baby with me? That's all I wanted, she said. She had loved me. Begged me.

What could I tell her? That I wanted someone to give my stuff to? Someone to carry forward the stories that had been traveling since the beginning of language. I stared at her. Said, You were right. This didn't help. She flushed, nearly plum. Asked me specifics. The woman. The doctor. The date.

When I told her, she began to laugh. Her mouth of teeth, wide. The trees shifted. The sun grew dark with clouds. Why would you bring another one of you back into the world, she asked, with all your anxieties and genetic shortcomings? I have mapped the road for him, I said. Unlike my parents, I have the manual. Can get him all the help in advance. She laughed. And laughed. Her voice in my ears. Sting and venom.

I had smacked her before I knew what I was doing. She stared. Rubbing her jaw. Her mouth a crack in her smooth face. She jabbed her finger into my chest. She said only, CLEARLY, and got into her car and drove away.

That night I sat under the stars. One fell. Crashed somewhere in the bluff on the far side of the river. There was maybe a hiss. The coyotes on the timberline ridge called. That lonesome croon that weaves itself between the trees and travels along the river valley to make bed in our ears.

The night had become a little darker. I thought of my ex-wife's last word. I thought of her new husband. Of their photos online. It'd be the bigger thing to find happiness in the fact that she found a man to give her what she wanted. Instead, I wanted him to come to some unexpected end. A fire. A gunshot. A comet coming loose from the sky and parsing him. I looked to the patio table I had built for my ex-wife on her birthday. I had bought the wood, uppacked the new saw from the box, and used an online for a guide to applying epoxy. It leaned in the moonlight. A ripple of uneven shell catching the light in jagged waves. Nothing like the well-balanced wedding bed my ex-wife's second husband made from a tree he'd hacked from the forest on the ridge beyond the river.

Slipping my toe on the corner, I lifted. I pushed. The table fell with a crack.

In the distance, a beacon of coyote eye emergged between the trees. The house light catching it right. It was unsettling, being stalked. Seeing the eye before hearing the breath and paw. I went to the garage. Pulled out the buckets of dog food. Lined them along the edge of the drive. Eased back into the house. They came. One at first. Two. Another. Until five gathered around the bowls. Sniffing, snarling, yipping. Their eyes fevered by the window light.

III.

On the day I was allowed take my boy home, I had that comingling of fear and excitement parents get on delivery day. While the boy was amassing in an incubation chamber, I'd had no worries. No panicked dreams. No thoughts of misshapen heads. Failing lungs. Blindness. I readied the house with little concern. Shopped for diapers with him in my mind as a thing and not a life. A life that could end for any number of reasons. Reasons that began to multiply in my thoughts. Crowding out words and directions.

It took me several attempts to arrive. Where I was meant to turn left, I turned right. Meant to stop, I accelerated instead, nearly killing a boy on his bike. What if my boy's hit while on his bike? Kidnapped. Molested. The world became so unbearable in that moment I can't remember arriving at the clinic.

I found myself staring at the glass door. A secretary came. Opened it for me. Are you okay? Is the door locked? I stared at him. Tried to say, *Fine. Open.* Finding instead the word *Abortion.*

They brought the boy to me. Swaddled in beige. A genderless color. As if they didn't know which he'd be. There they stood. Inches away. A baby sleeping in the crook of the scientist's arm. Here is your child, the woman said. Though my mind said *Move*, my hands remained locked at my sides. Sir, the woman continued. Then the boy turned. His pink lids a slice of flesh.

This I was not prepared for. Again, in theory, I had an image. *Child. Boy.* But never *Self.* He had my lips. My hair. The small birthmark at the tip of my right ear. An eelish feeling writhed in me. Between my ribs. Underneath. Swimming deeper inside. The scientist handed me the child. Her hands loose. A threat to drop him if I didn't take hold. The boy awoke when I touched him. His small eyes processing the compact fluorescents and dropped ceilings. I wanted to apologize to him. That his first visions were not of the trees and sky. That his first scent was not fragrant with the smell of pine along the trail by our house.

From what I read, I was to kiss him. To show him love. I pursed my lips. Bent my neck. But found myself unable.

Then. Then the boy reached up. His tiny hand a mess of fleshy nubs. So warm against my lips. Kiss. He smiled. I think it was a smile. It was familiar. Something I had seen on the old eight-millimeter films we found in my grandmother's attic. Me in my father's arms. Bouncing. Toothless. Happy. The film jumping. Burning at the edges. There was in my heart then a different stir. Not eel-like but gentle and glowing. Are you satisfied? the woman asked. I nodded and said something between *Yes* and *Uh-huh*. What will you name him?

I had spent days agonizing over this very question. Bought a book on names and origins. Scribbled notes in grocery store lines and in the middle of the night when I awoke from dreams and while watching movies. I had a name selected, a strong name, a name that was impervious to schoolyard puns. However, when I answered, I said, Leopold.

If I could have undone it, swallowed back the word before it reached the woman's ears, I would have. She smiled, looked at the boy, and said, Junior. There it was in my boy's head. A thing that couldn't be undone. He'd been named. If ever I thought I could change his name, the way I did so often with pets as a child, I knew then that I could not. It was different. Permanent.

I brought the boy home. Walked him along the path carpeted in pine. Dimmed in shadow. Smell, I whispered, this is the scent of the world. Feel the cool shade? His eyes were wide. Everything carving his mind. Engraving itself for replay in his dreams and later as adult as some pale memory he can't quite place.

Then I walked him through the home. I showed him all the rooms. Let him see the books. The art objects resting on shelves or tethered to nails. Took him to his room. Turned to show him the painted walls. I lowered him into his crib. Placed him on the pillow top mattress, nearly as tiny as he. He began to wriggle. His arms. His legs. A sea thing on its shell. Begging to be flipped right. I gently poked his belly. His pudgy arms retracted into his center and he smiled. Baby, I said.

When the boy had fallen asleep, I entered my office and began to peck at the keys. I carried numbers, divided, added, balanced. I accounted for spending, earning, manufacturing, distributing, rent. It was my singular talent. Balancing books in moments, what took others hours or days. In the books, the world was manageable. It was easy to isolate the anomalies and project future stock returns. Never had there been an error on my watch. Some nights I dreamed of people turned numerical. I lined them in columns. Subtracted those whom I found problematic. Multiplied those whom gave me hope.

Then. Then the funniest thing happened. I began to wonder what I dreamed of as a child but couldn't recall. It troubled me to the point that I stopped working. Walked upstairs where the boy slept and I watched him. Bent closely over his face as his eyes shifted beneath his eyelids. What did he have to dream? I hoped he dreamed of pine trees and fresh air and me and not of synthetic embryonic fluids, blinding white lights, or scientists. It seemed the child quit breathing for a moment. A strange electricity jolted through me. As if feeling it, the boy opened his eyes, turned his head to the side, and stretched his small pink hands. He then parted his lips, and from that small body, a shrill scream so fierce the windows rattled. My knees nearly gave out beneath me. How was such a thing possible? A primal bray so disturbing that my body wanted to quit me.

He didn't close his eyes. Stared right into me as if saying, You, yes, you are the source of my pain. I pulled him into my arms and he touched my face. Smiled. Made a gurgle of joy. I told myself it felt right. To be caring for the boy.

The child only slept occasionally and I'd use those moments to work. When he'd awaken, he'd scream. The house rattling. The light fixtures swaying on their chains. I'd rush upstairs, hold him, coo him. He'd smile. Laugh. Work at a language only he understood. I'd sit in a comfortable reading chair in the corner, the sun warm on us. Sometimes I'd nod off. The child would pull bits of me into his mouth. Gnash his gums together. Try to bite me. Suck instead. Sometimes it'd wake me, but when it didn't, he'd thrash and howl until the deed had been done.

He rarely slept and so it wasn't long before I began having trouble doing menial tasks and staying awake. I'd fall asleep warming formula. I'd nod off while sitting on the john. I'd collapse to the floor while tying my shoes.

I began taking the child into bed with me. We'd lay in the dark and I would wrap my arms around him so he wouldn't feel abandoned. This worked for a time, but as he grew, so did his demands. It wasn't enough that I was with him; he wanted me to talk to him, so I pre-recorded myself and put it on repeat. But he began recognizing the patterns in my speech acts. Then I recorded several speech acts and put the machine on random so that it would be more difficult for the boy to predict a pattern. This bought me two hours for a few days.

IV.

The boy was learning at an astonishing rate. He began collecting words. Perhaps I should've been proud, but each of the words he collected was slightly off. He would say *Lello*, for example, instead of *Yellow*; *Gree gree*, instead of *Hungry*; *Sold* for *Cold*. However, nothing cut me sideways as much as the word *Dabby*. It was as if the boy was trying to remind me of his artificiality. A dab of my DNA, a swab, the stab of a pin prick. Too, the boy was gaining weight at an alarming pace. Already he was twice the size of an infant. His squat limbs still too weak to carry his mass. His nerves not yet trained to crawl.

The boy's appetite was still growing. I was working through entire packages of formula in a day. As the hunger grew, his taste for the milk waned until he refused the bottle, so I tried to feed him with a spoon. With the edge of a bowl. With my hands. I consulted my books. One suggested I try using a prosthetic breast. I lumbered around the home with the harness strapped to me, the boy staring, his mouth opening and closing like a bass desperate for water. However, he would not eat.

Then. Then he began to make a new noise that sounded as if the tender fabric of his throat was being pulled from him. Raw and pink. He continued on like this for days. I tried baby foods, vegetables, fruits, and eventually candy. Nothing appealed to the boy.

At first, I refused to eat in solidarity. I found myself shaking with hunger as I rocked him in my arms. Baby, I said to him, baby, please, I'm so weak. So tired. Gree gree, he'd scream, the pitch a barb in my head.

I needed help but had very few people in my life. Most connections I'd made were through work. I'd moved to town with my ex-wife. She'd taken a job at the university. Over the years, my hometown friendships all but died. It was me and the boy now.

And so it was that I found myself calling my ex-wife for help. She was, admittedly, nonplused by my call. Please, I begged her, I don't know what to do.

I held the boy. Swayed him. Whispered those things I'd read one whispers to children. Eventually he fell asleep. The windows stopped rattling. I eased onto the couch. My arms weak from the weight of him. I fell asleep and dreamed of the boy towering over the city. Smashing through roofs with stubby feet.

Knocking over water towers, billboards, telephone poles. There was a woman calling to me from a building. He was about to crush it with his foot when I awoke to find my ex-wife leaning close to me. Speaking my name.

She remarked on the size of the child. Said, Jesus. Said, Massive. Said, House and home. Asked, Is something was wrong with him? I said, Yes. He's not eating. She put her hands around his waist. Tried to pull him free. The boy roused. His eyes wide in suspicion. Looking to me, he made a type of grin. I think. Let go. Allowed himself to be pulled to her. As if swaddling him, she rocked the boy in her arms. He, calm at first, bit down upon her. My ex-wife pulled her arm away. Looked at it as if it had betrayed her. Saliva upon the blade of her hand. Thank god he doesn't have teeth, she said.

Then. Then the child screamed. Unconditioned to the noise, my ex-wife jumped and the boy wiggled free, falling to the floor. Owie, he called. Dabby, he screamed.

He shrieked and the windows trembled and my ex-wife covered her ears. Looked at me with an expression, in all my years with her, I'd never seen. I suppose I should have felt anger. Yelled at my ex-wife for dropping the boy. But I didn't. Perhaps too faint from hunger. Perhaps too exhausted from the lack of sleep. I grabbed him but it didn't quiet his unrest.

My ex-wife began to back away. Toward the kitchen, her hands still high. She pulled paper towels from the holder. Wound bang snaps to fit in her ears. Shook her head at me before she pulled ground beef from my fridge. Pounded it into moon patties. Oiled a pan and began cooking. She stared out the window. Said, Jesus. I hate the way their eyes look. The coyotes.

They scratched at the back door. The bowls were empty. I didn't feed them today, I said. One of them howled. The boy looked at me. A smile emerging from the red face. I made a small howl. The boy imitated me. Then the coyote sang again. The boy imitated it. They're leaving, my ex-wife said. Will they come back? No, I said, it's doubtful.

My ex-wife removed the small burgers from the skillet. She brought them to us. A solar system on a plate. First, she handed me one. Said, you shouldn't feed meat to an infant, but maybe a little won't hurt. I pulled it to my mouth, but the boy snatched it. Shoved the moon into the pink toothless cave of his mouth. Gummed and swallowed. When my ex-wife attempted to hand him more, he recoiled in horror. She said, Oh, baby, and leaned in for another try. When she'd backed him into me, his head nearly vanishing into my armpit, he growled and lunged forward. Bit down her finger. To the start of the palm. Wiggling his head. A fish on a line.

She dropped the plate. The meat fell upon the floor. The once ordered planets spinning and falling and rolling under the couch. The child began howling. His arms stretched toward the fleshy orbs scattered at my feet. My ex-wife picked them up. No, she said, we don't eat food off the floor. The baby began to bray. He spat and hissed. He was strong. Much stronger than a baby should be.

My ex-wife stepped away. Dropped the meat in the garbage. Said that I could sort it out. That the baby was just as insufferable as me.

She looked out the window and then left.

I retrieved the meat from the trash. Fed some to the boy and took some for myself. As I gained a little energy, I pulled the remainder of the ground beef from the fridge. I sat the boy on the counter. Began to pound the cold pink strings into shape. But the boy took the raw beef into his hands. I tried to wrench it from him but was too late. It was in his mouth and gone. He smiled, reached for more. No, I said. Again the cries. The flatware rattling in the drawers. The lids on pots. Keys on hooks.

*

The boy could not be satisfied. His hunger growing. His restlessness. Never did he let me sleep. I'd close my eyes. Plug my ears. Sing to him. Rock him. He would carry on in his baby talk. Make wet lipped, spit bubbling noise. Reply to the coyote howls in the night. He'd become incessant.

The lines between day and night grew thinner until there was no difference. Until it was one long march of noise and fidgeting. Until I couldn't focus on work. Couldn't hold a thought.

I called the lab. Asked if any of this was normal. Asked if they had help. Anything. They need exercise, the scientist said. You need to take them out. They need stimulation. They're different than traditional children, she said. You must teach them connections. What do I do, I asked. Take your child to the park, she said.

The afternoon was ending. The sun growing closer to the horizon. I stood and gathered my keys. I packed some lunchmeats. Gathered the boy—who squirmed in my arms—searching for the bag of flesh. Not yet, I said. He growled a little. Showed his wet gums. We arrived at the car; I sat his fat body on the roof. Stabilized him with one hand and pulled meat with the other. Here, I said. And he grabbed it. The vacuum of his mouth taking it whole.

The boy was easy to buckle into his car seat. He patted his belly. Licked his hands. Sang something that was not quite a song. Some baby gibberish. Swooping hums and spit bubbles. He tried to touch me. To stroke my face. Dabby, he said. I pulled away. Said, I want to show you the river between here and there. I want to show you the ridge and the tall tall pines. The boy clapped. Said, Tines.

We wended through town. Descended into the valley. The sun strobing on the kid's skin. His face alight. Taking in everything. The world forming him as it scrolled by. He looked at me in the rearview. Smiled. As we passed beneath the iron wickerwork of a bridge truss, the child's mouth fell into a wondrous crescent. His eyes filled with the strange triangles.

The engine worked at the hill to the bluff. The expression of the boy's wonder tabled for a look of concern. Vroom, I said. He clapped. The world safe again. Vrooo! he said. At the precipice of the bluff above the river, I pulled to the side. The boy stared out the window. He hummed.

Click and release and he was in my arms. I carried him. Along the carpeted path of rusty pine needles. The shade cool. The world hushed. The smell intoxicating. Tines, the boy said. His head swiveling. Yes, I said. When I could see the river, I wove between trees. Found a small clearing where the last light of day slipped through in a soft slant. Warm and pleasant. I lay the boy upon a bed of pine.

He laughed. His legs curled inward. Pads touching. He grabbed fistfuls of needles. Tossed them overhead. Giggled as they rained upon him. Repeated. Bubbled spit and blew raspberries in the air. I stepped back. One foot at a time. Into the shadowed fringe. Another step into the black of boles. Dabby, the boy called. His hands no longer tossing needles. I could go. Retreat and not return. To sleep. Finally sleep. I turned away. Headed toward the car as night inched over the boy. His calls became more harried. I reached the door. Stopped. Grabbed for the handle. But couldn't. Couldn't leave the child.

V.

When the boy began teething, I had almost found myself asleep. His need had worn me thin. My body failing. My eyes unable to stay open any longer. As if freezing to death in September. I was drifting in that stream of almost sleep. And in that floating, a sharp pain came. First as a concept of white light, then as a sensation relating to my hand. I opened my eyes. Saw his gums. His lips spread in a sneer. The sharp edge of his tooth almost breaking the skin. So soon it had ripped through his gums. The tender pink of his mouth swollen around the blade of his incisor. I pulled my hand free. Got out of bed. Took the boy downstairs. Fed him some meat.

That afternoon I decided we would eat outside. If the boy insisted on eating meat, I'd cook it on the grill. Mix it with vegetables. Let the boy breathe the outside air before it grew too cool. Before the pine drooped with weight of snow. The sky low with clouds.

He was nearly too big for his highchair. Legs too wide, too long. The bucket seat tight on his ass. He could reach over his tray and touch the edge of the table.

I ignited the grill. I'd scarcely touched it since my ex-wife left. The thought of it painful. The nights with faculty drunk around the table. The smoke of meat low in the trees on humid summer nights. This will be a new start, I told the boy as I chopped a medley of vegetables—carrots, peas, corn. I stirred them with beef in a grand metal bowl. A fine mash rolled into balls. Pressed into thin discs. The boy thrilled in the burst of flame. The sizzle of meat. As I labored over the grill, the child grew anxious with hunger. Began slamming his hands. The plastic tray rattling in its cradle. But as abruptly as he began, he stopped—his eyes filled with curiosity.

A squirrel on a low hanging branch clucked at him. Squirrel, I said. The boy looked at me then to the squirrel. Rurl, he said. Yes, I said, Squirrel. I pulled a piece of bread from the loaf. Pieced it in a trail from the tree to the table so that the boy might see the squirrel better.

I tended to the meat. Flipping the patties every few minutes. I thought of the nest of squirrels that chittered in the mornings. How my ex-wife used to loathe them. Said they were up to no good. Called them brown rats. But I always liked them. Admired their ability to jump from limb to wire. To scale brick walls and stow away nuts and berries for a later date. Natural accountants, planning and saving. For the future. When the college students would no longer feed them. When the income of bread and candies would deplete.

I placed the beef and veggie patties before the boy. He pushed the top bun off. Sniffed at the brown disc beneath. Frowned. Looked to me then to the squirrel who followed my trail with circumspection. The boy smiled. Stretched his arms out in the way children do, their hands squid like in the air. Please, I said, my body slumped in exhaustion. Please, eat this. The boy didn't look back to me, so I returned to the grill and cooked a beef patty without the veggies. Pressed the bloody juice out with a spatula. Hiss and smoke.

This too, the child rejected. Sending it to the ground all spin and wobble. Before the squirrel could cross over to it, I snatched it. Put it on the table with the other the boy had refused. I returned to the grill and worked on making it rarer. A whisper came to my mind and it caught me off guard. Perhaps the boy craved the taste of blood. The thought of it made my skin feel loose. I hovered there, the heat of the grill inviting me to sleep. Caught between a dream and reality. How long, I thought, can a body continue without sleep? From the reverb of my thoughts, came the distant chittering of the squirrel behind me. The scurry of claws on the wooden table legs. The rattle of plates. My boy giggling with glee. Then. Then a shriek cut through me. My back. Muscles and nerves and spinal fluids rippling, rattling, shaking through me a primitive response. I snapped back to reality and turned. I turned with the spatula falling. Falling to the brick patio.

The boy had the squirrel. It thrashed and tore, leaving strings of jellied flesh along the boy's jawline. Yet the child didn't seem fazed. He tore at the animal's belly with his tooth. Viscera and fur dripping along his chin. Excrement and urine running down his neck.

As I lunged to free the squirrel from the boy's grip, the highchair fell. The squirrel landed several feet away. Scrapping along the patio, intestinal ribbons streaming behind.

The boy screamed. His oversized body trying desperately to crawl, but finding it too difficult. I stepped over the kid. Let him scream. Let him cry. Let his hands open and close. The sun on him angry and white. I stood above the squirrel, his small frame tremor and slide. His eyes closing to slits then opening to full black mirrors. I saw my foot in the reflection. Growing larger. As it connected with the head, the animal's back legs kicked in a last effort to escape. Then. Then the slow crush. The only mercy left.

I had the child in my arms. He protested. Bad dabby, he said. My, he said. My-My. I lay him on the kitchen counter. Treated his wounds. Hydrogen Peroxide hissed in the scratches. Phosphoresced on the bits of skin dangling along the edges. He did not cry. He pleaded for the squirrel. My-My-My-My! When I didn't respond, he bit down upon my hand. I tried to pull it free, but it was locked between bones. Blood swelling around the boy's lips. I swatted. I swatted and cursed. The boy only bit harder. I'll get the squirrel, I yelled and the boy released. Cracked a bloody smile. Clapped his awful little hands together.

I pulled the dead thing from the ground. Carried it back to the kitchen. Placed it in his hands. Slid my back against the cabinets and sat on the tiled floor. Wrapped my wound. Tender and dripping. The room was a whirl. The hum of fridge and suck and smack of the boy feasting. I closed my eyes and thought of the boy collecting animals. Eating them. The house reeking of putrefaction. The boy in preschool. Biting children. Eating them.

*

I must have been in that daze for some time. Slipped into slumber. Awoke to the voice of the child. The rattle of glass. The clatter of pots and pans. The kick of the fat-ridged legs. He'd eaten almost everything. Pulled the flesh and fur from the bone with an untaught dexterity. A sleeping gene passed into him from another generation. The bones, slickened with blood, on the counter, arranged in proper order. A map of his meal.

The sun had since gone down. The night hushed save for the call of the coyotes and the rattle of insects. The boy reached for me. Pointed to his leftovers. Pointed again to his belly. My, he said. Gree, he snapped. Then. Then he stopped silent. His head turned. The bay of the coyote. He laughed and mimicked the call.

My head, despite the sleep, was static. The nap only making more obvious my state. Exhaustion heavy and wet on my head. My eyelids so low they were nearly shut. I propped the back door open. Went to the garage and pulled free the dog food. I started to fill the bowls, but stopped short. Began walking back toward the door. Spreading kibbles along the ground. A trail. Back along the sidewalk. Up the steps. Through the door. Into the small breakfast room at the back of the kitchen. There, I stopped. Gathered the boy from the counter. Lay him on the floor. His fat limbs squirming against the tiles. I grabbed packages of meat from the fridge. Tore them free of plastic. Placed them on the floor for the boy to eat.

As he grabbed at the slices, I retreated.

Dabby, he called, his mouth filled with ham.

Then. Then I turned away.

I didn't look back.

Dabby, he called, a little louder this time. His feet shifting on the tile. Trying to crawl. Trying to follow. Dabby?

Outside I heard the panting breath of coyotes. I closed my eyes.

Dabby?

Without a word, I closed the door between the kitchen and the living room. Walked upstairs, closing every door between he and I. Lying down upon the bed. In the dark. Where I quickly felt the pull of sleep. The floating of body in that space in-between. The yip of coyotes as they gathered in the yard almost lost on me. Eat, I remember saying.

*

The following afternoon I awoke with a start. My body electric with the word *eat*. As if it had repeated in my dreams, each one louder than the previous. Until it was fervid white and hissing. Though I had strength, my body was still slow to stand. To walk even slower. Starts and fits. Back downstairs. Opening doors. Until I found myself outside the kitchen.

When I opened the door, I found one coyote. His body cold. The throat torn from it. The guts spilled sideways in a smear. Red paw prints, scratches on the walls, dabbed on the counters' edges. An epicenter of red violence in broad strokes where the boy sat. I tracked the trail outside. Found no trace of the child. I rounded the house. Walked the path I knew the coyotes took through the neighborhood. Stopped at the shallows of the river. No body found. There was in me a new barb cutting two ways at once. At one end an anchor, at the other a buoy.

I returned home. Cleaned the house. Pulled the feeders from the trees. Tried to return to my life. To numbers. To sleeping. And was able to. For some time. Avoiding calls from my ex-wife. Deleting her messages asking about the welfare of the boy.

Things were getting back to normal. Quiet. Orderly. Then. Then I saw the news. Heard the anchors laugh. Heard them say, it takes all kinds. I sat at on the couch, a fork full of tofu hovering inches from my lips. Something new working at me—far back in the parts of my spine I'd never cared to think about. Where all the bits come together. Fine bits of sinew wrapping bone into place. Coming undone.

I went to the basement. To the boxes. Unlocked my father's gun cabinet. Pulled one from the cabinet. The wood smooth, the weight of it terrifying. Unsure if shells went bad, I slipped some into the barrels. Clicked the body to. Brought it upstairs. Could I do it? Shoot the boy. I spent the day holding and not holding the gun. Wimbling on the choice. Before returning it to the case. Walking upstairs. Sitting on the couch. Watching the sun drain from the house. Dusk filling every corner. A pale light fell on the tile in the kitchen. A spotlight where the boy had killed the coyote. Where the coyotes did whatever they did to the boy. I sat there and waited. Night after night, I waited for my boy to return.

The Fine Set of Teeth

The tooth origins were unknown to him, but when he'd woken, disoriented from a dream he could not remember and went to the kitchen for a glass of water, Gavin found the tooth resting on the table. The tooth was spotless save for one thin string of saliva, which ran between the crown and the tabletop. Gavin scratched his left temple. The remaining strands of hair caught on his freshly chewed fingernails. The tooth had to belong to someone. He wrote a list of the people in the house: *Father, Mother, Claire, the Bible salesman.* He then wrote a list of the people who were not in the house: *Marie.*

He hadn't remembered seeing anyone missing a tooth. In fact, only hours before he'd remarked on the fine set of teeth the Bible salesman possessed. Gavin bent down carefully, trying not to displace the evidence.

He walked into the kitchen where the donut shaped fluorescent light flickered, quicker with each interval, until finally revealing the butterscotch floral pattern of the wallpaper. Making sure not to wake anyone in the household, Gavin crept across the linoleum to the tool drawer; it slid open with a wooden screech and the shelving paper filled the air with the stale aroma of rotting glue. He fumbled around, grabbed a rubber flashlight from the back, and walked into the hallway—his backless velvet slippers trundling against the hardwood floor, reverberating in the dark hall. At the last room on the right, he looked at his shoes, as if to silence them, and eased opened the whining door. He shuffled over to edge of the bed where Claire, her soft eyelids gripped tightly around sleep, lay in a fetal position . He squeezed his fingers between her lips to find all teeth present. She snorted and turned to her right. Gavin left the room and proceeded in this manner until he had checked the bedrooms. Everyone had a full set of teeth—everyone except the Bible salesman who was not in his bed.

In the living room, Gavin shone the flashlight over the eight-chair dining set, across the mantle, into the armoire, and paused. His mother had displayed her finest China in plastic brackets; the plates' gold edges shimmered in the flashlight's beam.

When Gavin was a child, his mother allowed him and Marie to wash the good china after special occasions. On his twelfth Christmas, he cracked one of the plates; Marie took the blame to protect him and was never again allowed to touch the china. Although it had been twenty years since, Gavin decided to thank Marie when she came home.

A gust of wind pushed a tree branch across the roof of the house. Instinctively Gavin raised the torch to the ceiling where it revealed someone had left the crawlspace hatch ajar. Pulling a chair from the dining room table, he placed it under the crawlspace, eased the hatch open, and poked his head inside. Inches away from the entrance sat a solitary napkin. Gavin picked up the paper with his index finger and pinky, pulled it down into the living room. It was identical to the white napkins they had used at dinner, pristine except for a single spot of blood in a smooth circle with one tentacle reaching toward the bottom left corner. This new development confused Gavin, as he now had two clues—a clean tooth and a blood drop on a napkin. He wrote a list of his evidence: *1 clean tooth in kitchen. 1 bloody tooth on napkin in attic.*

He returned to the bedrooms, inspecting everyone; however, this time he searched for blood stains on their hands but found none. He would have to climb upstairs and search for more clues.

In the attic, he shone the flashlight around the room. He had never been in the garret before as his father had never allowed him the liberty. Whenever Gavin or Marie had asked him, he'd replied, All the family heirlooms are up there, and I don't want you messing around and breaking things. Gavin had wanted to climb into the space before, but had always feared his father. Now, as an adult, he was damn well justified in his exploration of the attic. After all, he was doing the family a favor by tracking down the source of this mystery.

The roof slanted on both sides, but Gavin could walk erect through the center. There were several trunks with large black buckles lining the walkway. He tried to open two of them, but they required keys. As he searched, he noticed another room at the far end of the attic. Gavin squatted to get inside the short square room and found large foggy mirrors lined the walls giving the appearance of many flashlights.

The room was empty save for a baby blue rocking horse with brown hair, white eyes, black pupils, and bright red lips. Gavin hadn't seen this horse before, but remembered how he and Marie had often talked of owning horses of their own. They began to beg their father until one day, he returned home with a horse trailer in tow, a fine white horse head moving between the bars, eager to run free among the fields. Gavin ran his fingers down the painted mane of the rocking horse stopping just short of the seat; here rested two teeth—a pair of central incisors—soaked in blood. The perpetrator was getting sloppy. Gavin collected the teeth and left.

When he returned to the living room, he noticed a trail of blood he'd not seen before, which went in several different directions—most of which he'd already visited, but given the new clue, he visited again.

Sitting at the kitchen table, Gavin rolled the teeth in his right hand and realized he hadn't checked the basement yet. The basement, primarily used for laundry and his father's taxidermy business, was a dark and musty place Gavin tried to avoid. The animal heads and surgical instruments always made his stomach soft. Once Gavin's father dropped a freshly stuffed deer head down the steps; he retrieved the head, but when he walked into the kitchen with his latest piece of art, an eye was missing, so he sent Gavin down to collect it. There was something about that moment, the way the stuffed and mounted heads stared at him through the shadows damning him for an action he was yet to do, that made Gavin swear he'd never step foot in the basement again—and he hadn't until now.

In the laundry room, he pulled the string on a hanging light which swung about, throwing silhouettes and shadows around the room in a panic, exposing his father's studio in hot strobing flashes. The bulb from the laundry room proved just enough for Gavin to see his father's operating table and chair. He walked around the table and reached for the desk lamp but stopped just short when something crunched beneath his feet. Gavin turned on the lamp to find a carpet of dried maggots. His body jerked, knocking a few carcasses into his slippers. He turned to leave the room but a discovery kept him there: a trail leading to the wood paneled wall. When the paneling bent beneath his touch, Gavin wedged his right index finger between the cracks, pulled part of the wall aside, and found a hidden tornado shelter. Had he ever seen this room before? Perhaps, some a far-off experience he'd forgotten. He wondered why his father had concealed it. Did his father need a place to call his own?

In the room sat another rocking horse. This horse was similar to the first, but it was pink. The discovery posed a different problem as his father was of the opinion that toys made children lazy. Perhaps they belonged to someone else—family heirlooms. Running his hand down the painted mane, he found three more teeth and a swath of hair on the seat. He grabbed the evidence and walked back into the studio. The hair was black, which meant it didn't belong to the Bible salesman—his hair was blonde.

A memory came then, foggy and soft, he and his sister rocking on the horses as children, laughing. Then, from that a more concrete recollection of sneaking in on Marie brushing the white horse in the barn. He'd nearly forgotten how much she'd loved that horse, Poncho. Such a strange name for a creature so big. Stopping, his hand hovering there in the light, he remembered lighting a fire-cracker, the horse going wild. That couldn't be. He was sure he'd never seen the rocking horses before. He was sure of it.

As he set the tooth down, he realized there were no maggots on the teeth or hair, so he returned to the trail, following it to the far wall of the tornado room, where it crept beneath another slat of wood paneling.

Gavin pulled at the wall. Nothing. He felt around the edges. A cool breeze. Something was on the other side, so he ran into the studio to grab tools from his father's workspace. The tools rested (from left to right) in the order of largest to smallest, gleaming and polished without a streak under the light.

The paneling cracked open, and much to Gavin's surprise there was another room, a room full of rusty hooks and the smell of old metal. He couldn't see much but caught a glimpse of several animal shapes hanging from the hooks. On the popper nearest the front hung a loop of skin. Gavin pulled it free and returned to the studio, where to his horror in that low light, pale bloody lips hung from his fingers. Running to the stairs, Gavin's thoughts toggled, one moment trying to solve the mystery, the next remembering Marie lying upon the ground, Poncho bucking wildly, her mouth caved in from a hoof.

He checked the rooms again and found his mother, father, and niece were all missing; Gavin, now dizzy with anxiety, stumbled into the kitchen to find everyone sitting around the table.

Good god, exclaimed his mother, rushing toward him.

Gavin pointed to the Bible salesman, who stood in terrified silence, and tried to speak but realized he could not. Reaching to his mouth, he found it alien and slick with blood.

Peggy, call the doctor, Gavin's father said. He grabbed a towel off the kitchen counter and pressed it against Gavin's face as he turned to find his reflection in the storm door.

Gavin, his legs impossibly weak, stumbled and fell to the floor. The world fell silent, save for the pounding of Gavin's heart. Above him the light began to shine brighter, leaving the surrounding room black and silent, and in the distance, came the distinct sound of Marie humming.

The Father's Work

I. The Cat

When Cade killed his first cat, Boone sat the boy down and communicated the difference between inside animals and outside animals. The boy asked why they'd taken the blade to pigs if they were smart enough to be inside animals. Boone thought on it and reapproached the matter telling his boy there were some animals people ate and others they didn't. Running his thumb along the edges of his teeth, the boy asked why they'd killed coyotes if they weren't going to eat them.

The boy had a point and Boone found himself at a loss for words. He hadn't prepared for a conversation about life and death, but he had stumbled upon Cade whispering to himself while strangling a cat, then releasing it and grabbing it anew to repeat the process. So here they were, the boy looking to him for answers, and Boone wishing he'd chosen better examples.

No one had told Boone which animals to kill and he never told his eldest son Henry either. Boys on farms just understood. Why suddenly, Boone asked himself, did his youngest need this clarification? He couldn't fault his son for asking sharp questions, but when Boone had run out of examples, the boy finding fault in each of them, he said, Let's have a moratorium on killing unless I'm present. The boy agreed and that was the end of things. Until it wasn't.

When Cade killed a second cat, Boone found him kneeling over it, whispering in a secret language, knife in hand. If the boy had learned another language, Boone would have known. Perhaps, Boone thought, the boy's mother had taught him words from the old country. Once again Boone took the boy aside and asked him why he'd done it, and Cade replied that the cat had been suffering. Boone told the boy it wasn't his place to decide who was suffering. Then he asked the boy what language he was speaking.

It is God's language, Cade said.

No, it wasn't, Boone said, taking the boy to the shed to run a belt across his hide.

It was several lashings in before Boone realized his son neither cried, nor flinched, nor screamed. It was only after the flesh leeched, Boone ceased and said it was good enough, but something wound tight inside of him and he found himself unsatisfied with his punishment. He never had to take a belt to his eldest son, Henry. It was as if he'd been born to good. Thinking back to his father's punishments, Boone wondered if he'd missed something. Maybe from his vantage point he didn't see the punishment clearly enough to punish his own children correctly. Perhaps, Boone thought, he should bring the boy's grandfather over and let him punish the boy.

No, Boone had done the job just fine. Cade was, after all, bleeding. It didn't take a doctor to know he'd punished the boy too much. Then the twist came again, tighter this time. Why hadn't the boy reacted?

Did you learn your lesson, he asked his boy.

Yessir, the boy said.

That night he took Cade to the Dairy Queen on the edge of town. They sat on concrete benches out front and licked their spoons. The boy winced and shifted and the twist in Boone released, emitting a long sigh that was trapped somewhere inside.

Son, Boone began, what made you do what you done anyway?

The boy shrugged his shoulders, licked his ice cream, and said, It was suffering and I wanted to see what was inside.

Hell son, you've seen the insides of pigs, fish, deer, chickens. It ain't much different.

The boy did not answer. He stared at a toddler pulling at the fringes of her church dress. Lowering his ice cream from his mouth, Cade said, Why don't we go to church no more?

I suppose I ain't got the heart for it since your mother passed, Boone said.

He'd shielded the boys from their mother's slow death. The eldest had been away at agricultural school and Cade was too young to see his mother in such a diminished state. To them, their mother went to the hospital and would come back before they knew it. But she didn't come back, and though the eldest had asked about her, the youngest had stopped. After she'd hollowed out and died from lung failure, Boone took her to the funeral home, where the mortician did his best, but some things needed miracles, and the mortician was no miracle worker.

When it was time to put her on display, Boone thought it best to close the lid. There was no need for the boys to see her withered shell pumped with fluids and shellacked over in makeup. He began closing the lid when the pastor sidled next to him.

The boys need closure. Christ, Boone, we all do.

Have a look. Is that going to give anyone closure?

The pastor closed his eyes then spoke, It won't do them no good to lie. They'll have questions.

Goddamn it, Bill, they'll have questions either way.

Boone left it open and asked the boys to join him, where Henry took one eyeful and left the room. The youngest stared, his expression still. Boone patted Cade on the shoulder and went outside to attend to Henry.

Standing in the gravel lot, Henry lit a cigarette.

You should have said something, Henry said.

Wouldn't had made it better.

Boone wanted to tell his child something but knew there was nothing right to say. The eldest felt things the youngest didn't. Whereas the sight of their mother withering away in the hospital would have kept Henry up at night, Cade would have found a morbid curiosity in the details of their mother's illness. Lying to Henry tore him up something awful, but he couldn't risk the kid missing classes to be by his mother's side. There were too many days of slow dying there. Working up the right words to ease Henry's anger, Boone offered only, I'm sorry, Son.

Henry pulled a drag from his cigarette, held it there, and said nothing in reply.

The pastor rushed out, his shirttail undone, face red and swollen.

Boone, your boy, he said, come now.

Following the pastor, Boone found Cade standing before the coffin muttering again in his strange language, a small crowd gathering around him, stroking his shoulders and whispering. As Boone approached, he found Cade, touching his mother's body. First stroking her forehead, then trying to pry her jaw and look inside.

Pulling his son away Boone said, The boy is grief struck. Though there was no semblance of grief upon his face, Boone was certain the boy was grieving, even if he had a queer way of showing it.

As they left for the truck, Boone turned to the eldest and said, I need you to stay behind for the family.

I'm going back to school tonight, Henry said. He took one last drag from his smoke and returned to the funeral home.

In the car, Cade did not look at his father, and as they rounded the final bend of the winding country road, he said, You were gonna let mama suffer.

Boone smacked the boy, once from anger and once for good measure. The boy's head ricocheted off the glass with a sonorous thud. You don't speak to me like that, Son.

Cade adjusted himself, kept his eyes forward, and did not speak again for three days. Each time Boone would ask the boy a question, Cade would refuse to answer. Whenever Boone walked into a room, Cade would slink out, walk into the yard, and vanish for hours on end.

II. The Girl

Four days past the funeral, the neighbor's child turned up with rope burns on her neck; her parents came by to talk to Boone and he stood in the doorframe listening.

The boy always pays special attention to our girl, the father said, on account of her condition.

What condition, Boone said.

He'd known the girl was slow, but her parents had never told him about a condition. The girl didn't seem more touched than the slow folks who held jobs in grocery stores and feedlots. Seemed to Boone no one liked being slow, so people conjured up some condition to set them apart. The end result was just about the same.

Christ, Boone, you know our girl's brain didn't form right, the mother said.

This is news to me, Boone said. Damn unfortunate.

We were wondering if Cade saw anything.

Boone didn't have to ask Cade because he knew the boy had done it.

I'll have a word with the boy tonight.

Mighty nice of you, the father said and the neighbors left.

Cade returned home around suppertime. Setting his bike against the side of the house, he walked back to the shed, where Boone found the boy messing with a shovel.

What plan you got involves a shovel, Boone said.

The boy put the shovel down but did not answer. After they stood among sounds of bugs and livestock for long enough, Boone asked, What did you do that little girl?

Cade said, She is suffering.

You're going to get yourself strung up, son.

I can tell you I'll stop, the boy said.

Extending his hand, they shook on it and this was good enough for Boone, as surely the boy knew his father was not afraid to use discipline. The days followed with little incident. Boone kept his boy close and they tended the crops and managed the few pigs they had. As he watched Cade interact with the pigs, he began to see exactly how intelligent they were. Cade ran them through a series of routines and the pigs responded in much the way a dog would. Why indeed, Boone thought. When the day came to sell livestock in town, he did not. He lay in bed that morning weighing his options. They needed the money, but if he spared the pigs, showed Cade what real mercy looked like, maybe the boy would follow his lead. Yes, Boone thought, spare the pig, save the boy.

Cade entered his room, saw his father undressed on the bed, and said, We not going to town?

We're getting out of the livestock business, son.

This seemed to please the boy as he clapped his hands together and shook them twice. It had been some time since the boy showed youthful excitement, and if Boone was honest with himself, the boy had been forced to grow up quick once his mother passed.

Boone joined his son outside and Cade entered the pig pen where the animals surrounded him. Holding his arms spread as if hanging at the place of the skull with Christ himself, the boy said, You have been saved, and the pigs squealed in what seemed like celebration. Kneeling before a sow, Cade took her chin in his hand and began to whisper. The pig lay down, rolled to her side, and Cade left her there. The others wandered the pen and did not return to her side. She took three long breaths and went still.

When Cade returned Boone said, What transpired there?

She was sick and now she is gone.

Boone thought to ask the boy how he'd known the pig was sick, what she had and what he'd said to her that made her turn over like that. However, he feared the answers. Feared hearing his boy say some other strange thing to him that would require punishment. He was tired of punishing the boy. It was possible, afterall, boy had known the animal was sick and had just calmed her so she could pass.

That night, they supped on the back porch before turning in for the night. Boone hadn't been sleeping well, so he lay there thinking through the events of the day, finding the interaction between the boy and the sow increasingly odd. It couldn't have been the boy's words that brought that pig to her belly. If anything, she was happy for the affection, lulled into a sense of calm by Cade's tenderness. Boone was sure the boy had understood the lesson and the tightness in his gut loosened a little more.

As Cade and Boone settled into a new routine—the father tending crops with a careful eye while the boy wandered the woodlands—Boone's reservations about the boy left him. In the evenings, Boone would start a fire in the pit and Cade would drink a soda and listen to his stories. Cade always wanted to hear stories about his mother, and Boone was happy to share them. Life, it seemed, was back to normal and Boone began to sleep better. Some nights, though, he awoke to the sound of Cade walking through the house, whispering to himself. Perhaps, Boone thought, the boy was simply sleepwalking.

One night he woke to the boy whispering in the corner of the room. There he crouched down among the corner shadows, speaking words Boone could not understand. Easing out of bed, he took the boy downstairs and warmed milk over the stove. The boy was not interested in the milk, so Boone explained it would help restlessness. Cade said he was not restless and went upstairs to sleep.

A few days later, the neighbors stopped by again and asked if their little girl had gone somewhere with Cade. Boone had seen the boy leave that morning but hadn't asked where he was going. Boone told his neighbors this and they asked if he'd keep an eye out for their girl. That night the girl did not come home, so the neighbor's called again. Boone volunteered to search for her and this proved a kind gesture to send them back home.

Along the forest boundary road, he found his boy walking along the trees' edge, covered in dirt and bleeding from the cheek, the shovel swinging loosely from his hand. As the boy got into the truck, Boone asked how he'd hurt himself.

Helping a friend, Cade said.

Which friend, Boone said.

You don't know them.

Have you seen the neighbor's girl?

Poor thing, Cade said, such suffering.

Boone's hands began to sweat. He wanted to believe Cade incapable of killing someone but couldn't shake the feeling his boy didn't know the difference between helping and killing. He imagined the boy luring the simple girl to the forest, striking her upon the head, and burying her in a shallow grave.

Maybe the boy hadn't hurt the girl. Maybe he was out getting into kid's stuff like digging for treasure or building damns. Again, Boone imagined Cade standing over the girl's body, whispering to himself. Guilty or not, the boy was headed for trouble. If Boone didn't stop his boy, someone would kill him.

At home, Boone led his boy to the shed, where he instructed Cade to rest his hands, side by side on the work bench.

I'll ask you once. Did you hurt that girl?

I did not, the boy said.

Did you help that girl?

I did.

Boone wondered what his wife would have done in this situation. She'd always been a soft touch, making Boone punish the boys, but neither Cade nor Henry needed much punishment before their mother had died. What would happen if he didn't punish the boy? He imagined his boy in cuffs, the neighbors turning their backs on them.

Boone pulled an axe from the wall and raised it over his head as the boy looked out the window. Hovering there, Boone thought of the boy's birth, of his wife's joy upon seeing his face for the first time, and then he saw the boy torturing the cat, the terror in its face as it struggled against the boy's weight, the horrible silence after its screeches stopped.

Spare the rod, spoil the boy, he said and swung the axe, separating the boy from his hands.

The boy did not scream, did not cry, he raised the arms before his eyes, and then fell unconscious upon the ground. Boone knelt, applied tourniquets, and cauterized the wounds with a blow torch.

The following morning, the Sheriff stopped by the house. Removing his hat, he said, Hate to bother you, Boone, but we'd like to ask your boy some questions.

What kind of questions you got to ask, Boone said.

Neighbors think he's the last to see their girl.

That's what they said, is it?

Girl didn't make it home yesterday.

Sorry to hear it, Boon said and ushered the man in, leading him up to the boy's room where Cade slept, his bandaged arms lying motionless next to him.

Cade suffered an accident a few days ago. He's been resting ever since.

The sheriff's face grew slack, his eyes sad, Hell, Boone, I'm sorry for the intrusion.

I asked the boy and he said he ain't seen the girl in some time.

Boone showed the sheriff out and returned to boy's room where he found Cade, sitting up, fully awake. It seemed impossible the boy could recover so quickly, but here he was, face full of color, his pluck returned. Perhaps the boy didn't feel pain. Perhaps he was special. No, thought Boone, the young were just more resilient.

The boy began to whisper again, so Boone sat by his side to listen. Cade stopped and said, You're suffering.

Boon stood up again and said, I don't need your help.

I'm suffering, Cade said.

You've been saved from trouble, Boone said.

Boone explained he'd paid his boy a kindness, removing temptation from his body. The boy did not see it this way. His father told him to think about it another way, had he hands, he'd be in county lock up. The boy, though not smiling, thanked his father.

Preparing food for Cade, Boone readied some steak from the icebox. As it sizzled in the frying pan, thoughts arose of cows in cages, crammed nose to ass, terrified and wild. In his youth, he'd seen the men in slaughterhouses delivering death blows, saw the terror in the eyes of the cow before it fell still. He wasn't sure why it had stopped bothering him, but it had. Standing there in the kitchen, he once again felt youthful empathy run through him. Lifting the spatula, the meat browning on the edge, he slipped it into his mouth but did not find the familiar allure of smoky meat; instead, the meat was bitter. Was this the taste of suffering? Boone tossed the steak, making the boy hashbrowns and vegetables instead.

For the next few days, Boone cooked for Cade, and each day he'd find more unbearable suffering. At first it was the meat, but then eggs, milk, and cheese began to haunt him. He couldn't help but hear the boy's voice in the back of his head repeating the word *suffering* as Boone sliced, poured, and cracked. On the days he did manage to make food, the boy did not care to eat it. Boone moved the fork this way and that, like he did when the boy was small, but Cade turned his head, locked his lips, and mumbled, I won't eat like a baby.

That night as Boone lay in bed staring at the ceiling, Cade's footsteps echoed through the halls: step, whisper, step, whisper. What was the boy saying? Boone could not tell. Each night after, the boy paced and whispered and each time his voice became more pronounced. Still, Boone only understood one word: suffering.

Boone started to hear Cade's voice in his head. Sometimes it whispered and other times it pealed. Aware that a mind busy with lyrics offered little room for intrusive thoughts, Boone began to sing. On the days Boone attemped to apply pesticides or till the earth the boy's voice screamed in his head and Boone couldn't find it in himself to continue.

Once the boy felt better, the pain abating, he walked out of the house without speaking a word to his father and left. Boone rose from the couch to follow the boy but was not quick enough. He walked down the road, searched the shed, and drove around for a spell but could not find the boy.

This pattern continued for several days, before Boone blocked Cade and gifted him with a stash of comic books he'd bought at the general store. If Boone could distract his son, give him some youthful pleasures to keep him from finding trouble, he might just save the boy from his impulses.

Son, Boone said, I got you some comics.

Lying them upon the floor, Boone opened the first page of a comic with a plane flying low over soldiers in uniform. The boy took a knee and wrestled with the page until he was able to turn it. Boone left and Cade whiled the hours away in the livingroom, using his forearms to turn the pages, often flipping each comic over to start again after he finished. At first, he struggled with these tasks, but soon enough the boy moved about the pages as if he'd been born without hands.

III. The Stranger

One day while breaking ground on an unused portion of the field, Boone hit a rock with his sledgehammer and lost control. He tried to dodge the ricochet, but the hammer knocked him out. When he came to, he was beneath the stars, the world spinning before going still, In the distance, the house sat in darkness. He stood, leaving the sledgehammer behind, and walked home.

The house was filled with shadow, silent save for the sound of a lone cricket. Cade was not home, so Boone waited for him, and as hours passed and the sun began to rise, Boone got in his truck and began searching anew. Along the backroads and town streets, he drove with a careful eye lest the boy should see him and hide. Despite his doubling back, Boone could not find his child.

Eventually the boy returned—his boots gone ruddy in the toe and throat. Without speaking to his father, Cade walked into the bathroom, kicked his boots into the tub, and used his toes to work the facet.

That'll ruin them boots, Boone said, they ain't been treated yet.

The boy did not reply, only moved the boots around in the dirty water, trying to rinse the blood from them.

What you been into, Boone said.

His son turned to him and said, I was helping a friend.

Boone didn't know what Cade meant by this and didn't ask

before setting upon him with fists until the boy lay next to the tub, unconscious. Leaning over Cade, Boone asked if the boy was playing pretend, but he did not answer, so Boone checked his pulse. Then, with his hands under his boy's armpits, Boone lifted him and took Cade to the shed, where he lay him upon the workbench. Even with no hands the boy had found trouble. If his legs had taken him to trouble, his salvation lay in immobilization. With only a few moments to act before the boy came to, Boone grabbed his hatchet and began the hard work of a good father. When the leg did not give on the first swing, Boone tried again, this this time waking the boy. On the third swing, the leg came free, and Boone reached for his blowtorch but could not reach it. The boy struggled against him, so Boone pulled his belt from around his waist. As he tried to wrap it around, the boy punching and kicking, Boone resorted to knocking Cade out so he did not bleed to death. Slipping the belt over the thigh and cinching it, Boone stopped the bleeding and earned himself just enough time to take the boy to the hospital.

The nurses at the hospital asked Boone a litany of questions and he responded with the following answers: a few minutes ago, trapped under a tractor, hatchet, and finally just plain bad luck. They wheeled Cade into surgery, and a nurse escorted Boone to a room with an empty bed, where he remained until Cade returned from surgery—not to tend crops, the pigs, or shower.

On the second day in the hospital Cade was more present, so Boone said, Do you know why I done it.

The boy nodded.

Patting Cade's good leg, Boone said, If the good Lord can't chase these compulsions from you, I will help him.

That night Boone dreamed of removing Cade's limbs. With each limb he cut, another grew. Somehow the boy broke loose scampered away like a bug. Boone pursued him and found Cade, pillow in his arms, hovering over his mother's head.

Boone awoke in a sweat, his legs tacky against the faux leather of the hospital recliner. What had the boy meant when he'd told Boone that he was going to let his wife suffer? Had the boy relieved his mother of suffering? Boone did not know, but when he rose to ask the boy, he found his bed empty and the wheelchair gone.

Finding a nurse in the hallway, Boone asked if they'd taken his boy for tests, but the nurse could not say.

I can call the orderlies, she said.

Don't worry, he said, the boy likes to wander.

But the boy has no leg, she said.

The boy has stubborn fortitude.

Searching the hallways, peeking in rooms, Boone could not find Cade. When he finally made it to the rooftop, he found a stranger balancing on the edge of a small wall running along the edge of the building. Just below him, Cade sat in his wheelchair whispering to the stranger. Boone called to his boy, but Cade did not answer. The stranger placed his hands on his ears and began shaking his head, no no no. An angry pucker of stitches ran along both the man's forearms from a failed suicide attempt. Boone called to the stranger, and the man, face bunched and pained, met his gaze before taking a step forward and falling from sight. Boone rushed Cade out of the hospital and helped him into the truck.

What did you say to him?

The boy did not answer. Boone put his hand on the boy's shoulder and said, How can I protect you if I don't know what you really done?

He was suffering, Cade said.

There was partial truth to this; after all, Boone could see the suicide attempt right there upon the man's skin. Had it been for show, he reasoned, the man would have cut laterally below the palm. Still, Boone wondered what his boy had said, so he asked again, and this time the boy answered, the language of compassion.

It wasn't for another week before the police came around again, this time asking if Cade had been on the hospital roof. When Boone informed them his boy had not been on the roof, for his boy had lost his leg in an accident, the sheriff asked if he could see the boy, and upon seeing Cade lying in his bed with his leg wrapped, asked Cade if he was okay. The boy did not answer.

A man at the hospital jumped off the roof today. Orderly says he seen your boy only moments before.

How many moments exactly, Boone said.

The how many ain't important.

The orderly was wrong. Cade never left his bed until I put him in his chair and rolled him out.

The sheriff asked Boone to step outside the boy's room for a moment and as the two stood there among the shadows of the hall, said, It strikes me funny we have two incidents where people claim to seen your boy.

Cade ain't guilty of nothing but bad luck.

I ain't sure that boy has bad luck at all. The sheriff looked back to Cade then to Boone. His eyes slitted and he said, We ain't done, Boone.

That afternoon, Boone went to the drugstore to get the antibiotics and pain killers the doctor had called in. After the pain medication put Cade under, Boone went to the shed and returned with scissors, pliers, and his blowtorch. Cade slept soundly as Boone eased his tongue from his mouth. It wasn't the pinching or the cutting, which woke the boy, but the flame. Again, the boy did not cry, just sat there with the root of his tongue moving about helplessly in mouth.

As Boone fell to sleep, he dreamed of Cade crawling atop him, his mouth open, a choir of angels singing within. Awaking in a hot sweat, Boone checked the boy's room and found him lying there upon his back, biceps spread and rowing, eyes rolled into their lids where in the cool light of dawn they glowed unnaturally, his lips moving without sound. Then his words formed inside Boone's head, each one louder than the last, and as they grew louder, becoming more clear, he understood they were not just the words of his son, but the pain of all things suffering world around him, all speaking out in agony—the chick who fell from the nest and sat half-baked to the sidewalk, the pigs whose stomachs raged with hunger, the child whose limbs ached and whose throat sat dry. If only Boone could stop it. Could take back the curse which first plagued his child and now him.

Sitting by Cade's side, Boone lifted a hand to wipe sweat from Cade's brow. He placed his mouth by the boy's ear and whispered, I'm here to help you, my child.

Mother, I Have Dreamed of You

1.

When she awoke, it was to her daughter standing in the hallway, posture rigid, hair flooding her face, singing in a sweet but alien voice, *The children sleep beneath the bed*; at first, Candice, thought it a dream, the way her daughter hovered there in her tiny nightdress, the glow of a soft wan moon slung in a ribbon across her chest, but as the fog of sleep waned, her daughter's figure solidified, and Candace called her name. The girl turned, eyes fixed on some distant thing, and she blinked.

Liza, she called again, but her daughter didn't wake, only turned on her heels and walked to the end of the hallway where she knocked twice on the window and lay upon the floor.

Candice rushed to Liza and shook the sleep from her.

I had a bad dream, her daughter whispered, I don't want to sleep in my room.

They crept back into the master bed and Candice held Liza until both fell asleep, waking only when the sun rose.

2.

I dreamed of children born of cane fires and blood, their cries running a gryke in the limestone moon hanging scythe-like in the late-night sky. Their limbs knotted in the flash of fire and shadow, slick and tender. When I sought to untangle their oh-so-many-limbs, I found their skin loose, sloughing away beneath my fingertips, their cries escalating into a dizzying pitch. Then the world fell dark and cold and there was only the smell of ash.

3.

Liza and her mother sat upon the screened-in-porch just beyond the once used conservatory with its broken pipe organ. Can we fix the piano? Her daughter howled every time they passed the music room. Please, she would add for dramatic effect. Maybe someday, Candace would promise, but such opulent reminders of her family's past did not need reconditioning. As Liza combed the her doll's hair, a memory came to Candance of her great-grand father playing that organ, its angry voice racing through the halls of the mansion, the servants pacing with haunted looks upon their faces as if the melody reminded them of their parents' suffering in the fields—those long hours beneath the sun, the whip biting at their backs.

I've met a girl, Liza said.

Did you now?

In the yard. A small girl with a brown dress. She's very pretty, mommy. As Candice turned to find the girl, Liza said, You won't see there, mommy. She doesn't like the sun.

72

We should invite her over for a slumber party some time. A real girls' night. Would you like that?

Liza nodded her head emphatically and began to comb her doll's hair again.

4.

I dreamed of the hot sun growing larger until the sky was nothing but fire and the strange green plants around me burned sweet and hot, until my skin began to grow dark and wet. A girl in a metal mask emerged from the flames, her hand held high before a thin whip of flames stuck her down and the world fell dark.

5.

Liza had been floating in the swimming hole, crystalline spring water winking in the sunlight, and then she wasn't. She had vanished into the awful black depths of that pit. How it changed the world when below the surface—the hole Candance had swum in as a child, sunbathed next to as a teen, skinny-dipped in on drunken nights. Jumping in, her feet tightly pressed to a point, Candace sank deep into the hole's throat, until she was nothing but a ghostly waving figure and then, she imagined, nothing at all. How long had it been? How far had she gone? The light above grew dimmer, and as she moved along the curve of the wall, into the turn of the cave, light was nearly snuffed. Had it not been for the pink florescence of her daughter's goggles, she may have missed Liza, her limp body barely visible in all the cave's gloom. Slipping her fingers under the straps of the suit, a suit that had seemed impossibly small when she'd bought it, as if she had never been a child herself, Candace tried to pull the lyrca from a blade of stone, but it wouldn't detach. Had she'd not known better, she'd have insisted small hands were trying to keep her daughter there, deep below the sunny plantation. As air began to push desperately to leave her lungs, and sa white glow formed around her vision, she thought she saw the small black face of a child peeking from the stone. Pulling hard, she freed Liza and a small trail of bubbles began to trail from her mouth.

The glassy surface had never felt so distant, the world so unreachable. Candace cocked her legs against a slant of smooth rock and launched her body toward the light. It wasn't enough, she clipped her legs together, cutting water (much too slowly) until she was closer to the sun's warmth, each clip a little warmer. When she'd all but breached the surface, panic set in, the idea of glass trapping them, like in that movie she'd seen, the one with a white cat and splayed hand. Almost out of breath, she yelled to expand her chest, and as she did, the world greeted her and she and Liza were born again into the green beauty of the world.

6.

Before the dark took me, I saw them again, heard them calling, their sing-song voices seductive, *closer*, then, *keep us from sinkin' down*, until I came around the bend, until I found the dark. I saw their burning eyes and slipped into a dream again, the world of fire and ash gone. It was cold there, cold and dark. *Speak*, they said, and so I did. My words were no longer sharp and angular, but were round and percussive, and with each I felt pressure on my chest, a foot, a hand, a head. Then there was nothing. No feeling at all. Only a long cold silence. *This is death*, I said but no one was there to hear it.

7.

Candace found her daughter in the yard with a small trowel, a strange fey look upon her face as if she were not herself. The late summer air was cooling and fireflies punctuated the pre-dusk shadows with hopeful light in the gathering darkness below the trees. The curved edge of the shovel sparked against something hard. Liza traced her fingers around a shape in the clay and then eased the shovel beneath to wedge free a large iron circle. It was as if she knew where it was, how to dig it up.

Sweetheart, why are you digging here?

I'm searching for treasure, Liza said, holding the metal loop up for her mother to inspect. A link from a chain awkwardly jutted out, rusted into a permanent still of falling. I found a necklace.

How did you know to start here? Her mother said.

The girl shrugged.

Looking around the field, her mother asked, Did someone tell you to dig here? Was it miss Linda or mister Elijah?

No.

Anyone?

Liza shrugged and inspected her treasure. There in that dull light so desperately trying to stay day, Candace pulled the iron restraint from her daughter and said, Let's put this away and look at it in the morning.

In the house, Candace placed the rusting artifact in a draw and walked Liza to her bathroom, where she started the water. You have to take a bath now. You're filthy.

How much do you think my necklace is worth? The girl asked.

Oh honey, I don't think it's a necklace. I think it was for the livestock years ago.

Stepping into the water, Liza shook her head and said, She said it was treasure.

Who?

My friend, Liza said, squatting down into the water, easing one leg out at a time to sit.

Candace sat on the edge of the old clawfoot tub, washing her daughter the way her mother had washed her, and the way her mother's nanny had washed her mother, traditions changing with time. The house was filled with memories of these traditions. Some of them tender like this, but many painful and embarassing. Maybe she would sell the house to men who'd wanted to build a country club there, but the idea didn't sit right with her—thinking of the sprawling fields with its many white fences and gay thoroughbreds running through the mists.

Liza played with her bath toys, moving Manhattan Sandy through the bubbles. Then she turned towards the bedroom door and said, Downstairs.

What's downstairs, honey?

Liza smiled at the door for a moment, and as if snapping from a trance, looked at Cadence and said, Oh nothing.

8.

I dreamed of another body. Wet and burning. Then cold and forgotten. I dreamed my lungs burned with the screams of another. Then of a dark night and digging and falling down a long shaft. I dreamed of ashes and the sweet aftertaste of sugar. I dreamed of sleeping, of my chest forever still and forgotten.

9.

The night before Liza's tenth birthday, Candace awoke to her daughter missing. She was neither in her bed, nor by the window overlooking the back, nor on the couch in front of the television, nor in the sunroom, kitchen, nor one of the oh-so-many bath-rooms in the aging mansion. A cold finger of panic scratched along the backside of her ribs and then the image of the swim-ming-hole's mouth floated from the back of her thoughts—its tightening passage snaking behind. She ran onto the sundeck, past the stone guest house, and toward the hole. Liza, she called. The cruel shot of her own voice echoed back at her. Behind her, came the dull monotone voice of her child singing again, *The children sleep beneath the bed.*

In the thatch of night, Liza's white gown, a ghostly apparition sway-ing in the breeze appeared, seemingly disembodied in the darkness. As Candance grew closer, she saw her daughter, once again standing impossibly still, in a dream trance, staring down at the guest house's foundation. Liza fell to her knees, screaming, a raw and otherworldly voice tearing through the hum of crickets. Digging with her fingers, the clay coming up slowly (pulling the girl's nails backward) she howled, They can't breathe, they can't breathe. Candace scooped Liza up from the earth to find her small gown rusty from earth and blood, claggy from sweat.

My baby girl, she said, her voice crackling with confusion, who can't breathe?

Liza motioned to guest house, eyelids cut across her eyes, cruelly, and said, The little girls.

10.

Sometimes when I awoke, I was in a different room, my small body damp with sweat. On those days, my feet hurt and often times I found cuts or bruises on my skin. The dreams would stay with me until I began dreaming awake.

11.

The next evening Liza returned from the doctor's office, her hands bandaged, her voice gone, Candance fed her sweet strawberry ice-cream and they watched *The Battle of the Network Stars*. It had been a long day of scans and tests and they were both tired, barely making it through the episode. After she put her daughter to bed, Candace sat in a rocking chair and watched Liza until they both succumbed to sleep. She dreamed of Liza slipping into the mattress, of small hands, of fire. Then she roused to a room filled with smoke. The bed aflame. Choking, she rose to save her child.

Stepped to snatch her small body from the flames, but found only a searing hole, found heself burning, her hair whispering away into embers, her eyelashes curling hot into her eyes. Then she felt small ashen hands pulled' her deeper and deeper still until it seemed she was well into the earth, until she began to hear the honeyed voices of children singing, *We'll stop up de cracks and sew up de seams, Oh, go to sleep and dream sweet dreams.*

12.

I dreamed of my mother, away in a distant fog, creep-crawling into a hole where she slunk down, her serpentine legs whipped to a point, and then I dreamed of flames and a stench of burning hair. I dreamed of her singing a song, and when I awoke, she was no longer in the chair. In the house. No longer anywhere.

Nonconcentric

The next time he'd see his father it would be in a plastic box. Quartered out by the spoonful. No longer a body but a thing. A recipe. But this wouldn't be the last time he'd see the box. He would see it daily. On the shelf in the office. Light reflecting off the tape. A bag inside. Filled with ash. Ash for skies. Ash for water. Ash for dinner.

☐

Some days there wasn't a memory of his father. Only the box. A thing. Books propped against it. The memory of the man erased. Or obfuscated. The box on the beach in the 80s. The box in the Cadillac. The box sitting next to his scrawny body as he rattled with fever saying, There, there, son, you'll be well. The box watching him swim. A boy and his box.

☐

Outside nothing changed. The sun rose. The storms came. The insects seeped from the earth and slithered. They crawled. They sang their unholy songs. The house settled as it had before. No haunts. No specters to remind him. To resurrect the shape of his father. The thought of the ghost brought him comfort. He looked for it year after year. Knew what he'd say. To comfort the restless father. But that visual too began to change over time. First the hands pixilated. The feet. Quickly along the arms, up the legs, until block-by-block, he was square. The box hovering between the rail and the wall. Along the hall in the basement.

☐

It seemed to him that the world should be somehow visibly changed. The sun darker. The grass paler. Something. It was unfair that it could live unchanged. That the bugs could sing. The sun could shine. He stared at the box. Thought of the other boxes. Clustered in his brother's storage unit. Labeled and forgotten. The other siblings finding it too morose to take their boxes home. He finding it too much to take all of them. Too many pieces to remember. To litter about the house.

☐

There were times when he still reached to call his father. To tell him how hard life was. On Father's Day, he would stand over the box. A drink in his hand. A toast. You'd be proud, Dad. I've arrived. The box did not answer.

☐

Girlfriends would come into his life. Cohabitate. Ask him during spring cleanings. What's in here? What's that? Do you need this thing? Would you like to buy better bookends? The box sat silent. Once he placed his ear to the box. Whispered, whadaya think of her?

☐

He'd watched a movie with his father as a boy. Shortly after he'd struggled through the fever. There had been a black box. Slender. Tall. It descended from the sky. Presented itself before the apes. That, his father said, is something. *Something* he thought, leaning his head against the box on the sofa. His neck still weak from the fever. The apes were driven mad. They screamed and slammed their creepy bald hands.

☐

He walked to the shelf and grabbed the box. What was that movie, he asked. The movie with the box. Was the world showing him a secret? Did his father know all along that his world would become a box?

☐

It occurred to him. He too would be a box. But no one would hold his box. No books resting against him. No space to house him. A box somewhere else. A box without a home. His name, perhaps, written upon its lid.

☐

He began seeing himself as a box. A box graduating from college. A box losing his first wife. His second. Teaching students. A box growing old in an empty house. A box standing before a box. The world around him as it was before. The shadows long and shallow. The lights lemon or beige or gold. He could never tell.

☐

That is what the film was telling him. Or the box was telling him. Or he was telling himself. All the world a box. Each one lighter than the previous. Each one cared for until there was no one left. And they would stand. Stand in cities of vacant homes. Testaments or corpses or messages or props. Things placed on shelves. Stored in garages. Divided. Carbon in bags in boxes. Replacing everything but the world outside. The world that never changed. Where apes scream. Others rattle and slither.

Part II

The Light for Both of Us

It was on the third year of executions that you and I renewed our vows. You had been so hopeful. You said no economic or political collapse would chase from us those elements of humanity that made us unique, even after The Breakdown, when the infrastructures began to fail, bridges collapsing, reactors failing, police forces defeated, when we ran out of fuel resources, when people began burning whatever they could to stay warm, starting with wood and paper, and moving to plastics, chemicals, and fabrics. When the gangs came through our home, beating me, robbing us, pulling you into the yard to abuse and humiliate you, you pulled yourself together, mended your wounds, stitched your clothes. You said, We are only stronger for having survived. Our love is a light that never burns out. We had a vow renewal ceremony among our surviving friends (who seemed more baffled by your optimism than by The Breakdown itself) on the furthest reaches of our sector, where the trees stood, the leaves weighed down by black ash. When the winds came, they briefly parted the pitch sky and we could see, for a moment, a pale orb of sunlight, obscured but present. We stood in silence until you said, Our love will last as sure as that sun shines, and we kissed, slipping new rings fashioned from cans, hammered and polished, upon our fingers.

—

This was before the rains changed. Before the dogs began to turn, starving and mad. Before the carcasses of cats, then children, began appearing beneath bushes, pale and slimy, their eyes white and velveteen. Before the first reactor began to leak and poison the earth and kill the children. Before women lost their hair and men found themselves impotent. Before the gangs took total control of the towns. Before people began trading their dead for fuel to burn. You were in the garden when you first noticed it. The brown viscous rain drops. Some tore through the kale. Your garden began to wither. The things you saved, we tried cooking, but they made us sick. We began trading what little we had for canned food. You told me I looked thin. Tired. But I could see it was you. After the rains, a part of you was gone. Maybe you started seeing what the rest of us had seen long ago. The inevitability of it all.

The neighbors joined an end-of-days cult. They began having meetings. The preacher spoke late into the nights. More and more people joined them. We found trouble sleeping. I asked them to stop. I swathed myself in plastic, slipped shop goggles on my eyes, wrapped a scarf around my mouth, and walked through the brown drizzle, made black by night, and said, Please, my wife has grown so frail. She needs rest. They would not. Soon I grew too tired. My tolerance thin. I struck a man on the cheek, my blow an eighth of what it had been when the world was green, when I woke before the sun to build homes, when the hot sun still burned skin. How I complained about those days. Sunny days won't last forever, you said to me, your way of ensuring I took nothing for granted, fully aware of how unaware I was. The crowd fell upon me. Pounding me with their fists and their metal crosses. If I'd thought there was nothing left to hurt in me, I was wrong. My skin breached and blood poured from me in angry torrents. Had a roving gang not arrived and clashed with the fanatics, I'd not have crawled home. Alive, but barely. You rolled over and found me, breath rasping through my throat. Death lowering my eyelids. I remember waking as you treated my wounds. Using the remnants of our first aid kit. Laying pieces of your shirt over my wounds. I wanted to tell you to stop. To save your energy. But I was weak. Too weak. By the time I was well enough to stand, you'd been awake for days. Worried, you said, that I wouldn't come back from it. That you would be left alone.

For a while, the rains came more frequently and then they ceased altogether. We were thankful at first. You hoped it would give the earth time to heal. But the rains never returned. Neither clean nor dirty. Those plants that had survived, died in the drought. We had heard rumors there were parts of the country where they could still grow plants, still harvest food, where dogs weren't eating each other in the streets and where gangs weren't pulling apart houses for firewood. But no one had proof of this.

People in our sector ran out of things to trade. For fresh food. For clothing. What had once been a suburb had become a collection of hovels that only offered protection as long as the gangs hadn't dismantled them. Those without homes, left. We didn't know where they went. They didn't say goodbye. People with whom we'd grilled. People we'd helped with graduation parties, birthday parties, weddings. People we'd loaned tools and sugar to. All gone without a word.

Some days I thought you had come back. You'd sing a fragment of a pop song you'd once loved or tell a joke. You'd ask me if I remembered a television show, the one you liked with the skinny woman who married the bumbling fat man. But then you'd go away. Your eyes seemed to go dull and your cheeks hollow. I'd touch you. Stroke the back of my hand along the cut of your jaw or clavicle or arm. You were unmoved. It was like I was air. Or something less.

We received word other countries were organizing relief efforts. Refugee camps. Displaced Persons programs. Israel had shut its doors to us. Cuba had initiated non-stop water patrols to stop our kind from crossing the ocean. China had attempted to help but found the effort too costly. They left some military reserves to help evacuate areas around leaking reactors. When that was finished, they left. Russia and Brazil pledged money for supplies. Ireland offered sanctuary for first and second generation Irish. You and I had nowhere to go. I asked you if you wanted to travel to the ocean and build a boat. To push away from our shore and attempt to drift until we found refuge. Perhaps some fishing crew would rescue us. Some island might take us. You said, No, we are far too weak to survive more than a day at sea. And what if the rains return? You were right. You usually were.

When the UN arrived to help quell the gang violence and erect refugee camps, we stood in line. Look, I said, this is hope. You didn't answer. You made to nod, but you were so frail your head fell and struggled to return upright. I helped, rubbing my fingers over your bare scalp that had once grown platinum hair, smooth like some impossible piece of moonlight. My hair had fallen out before The Breakdown. When I was still young. When we'd first started dating. How you liked to tease me about it. Called me old man. Brought me toupees and gag miracle grow. And how you would laugh. That sparkling giggle that was more harp than voice. What I wouldn't give to hear it now.

When we made it into camp, the beans and rice and vitamins returned color to us. The purified water cleaned us. There were troupes of entertainers flown in to ease our minds. I had conversations with people from other sectors and we compared stories. Yet, it seemed the more I became human, the more you were reminded of how inhuman we'd become. Remember the time we went skiing in Switzerland, I said, when you woke up to find it snowing and told me the world was playing out in slow motion and we danced beneath the streetlight? I remember when you killed the cat and peeled back its hide, cut from it thin and stringy meat, you said. Remember the time your mother bought us those horrible matching windbreakers to take to Ireland on our honeymoon, I asked. Remember sitting in the house when the gangs took our neighbor's daughter? How we heard her scream? How we heard the parents protest? How we heard them die? When we did nothing to help? How we gave up fighting when they came for us? For me.

Maybe you were right. Maybe we were unable to return to what we had been. Maybe the crimes of survival were irreversible. The rest of us sat there acting as if nothing had happened. Too scared to remember what we were capable of. Too scared to ask, What's the worst thing you did? So, you and I fell silent. Days passed where we wouldn't speak. I brought you our daily rations and you let them cool, go bad, be carried away by rats. You lay in the cot and stared at the apex of our small tent. Some days I would do the same. Just to feel closer to you, like we were doing something together, like when we used to sit on the floor of the living room and listen to our old 45s.

When you ceased to leave the tent, save for using the latrine, I took to staying in with you. I traded some of my rations for a ham radio. As not to disturb you, I'd use an earpiece. On my side, I lay and watched the ridge of your face and listened to talk shows from foreign countries. They brought survivors and Displaced People on to tell their stories. One woman spoke about the men who raped her. One of the men, she said, punctured my eye. I'm blind in my left eye. The host asked her to show the audience. The woman lifted her eye patch and the studio audience moaned in disbelief. The host gave his apologies. It's not your fault, the woman said. It's humanity's fault, he replied. His answer was practiced. Even. As if he was simply ordering a meal. The woman then detailed how her husband killed the family pets to eat them. She cried more for the loss of the family dog than did she when detailing her attack. The dog looked to me, she said between pauses, as if asking me to stop it. What did you do, the host asked, but stopped her just before she answered and said, We will be back after a word from our sponsor.

I thought about killing our cat. I thought about his run from me. The brick I'd used to crush his skull. How much I'd loved that cat. I thought about how tough the meat was. Bland. You couldn't stomach it. You just let it sit there on the plate. I ate it later, cold. The host returned and rephrased his question. The woman said, I did nothing. I cried. I fed the meat to my boys. I told them a lie, but their father corrected me. Told them the truth. He said that the boys needed to know the truth to survive after The Breakdown. They are more like him. They ate the meat without question. My oldest son said, 'It's either us or them.' I prefer, she said, pausing for a moment as if she were gathering something from the air, not to make a choice, if that choice is death. With this, the audience erupted in applause. Well said, the host cheered, well said, indeed.

You began sneaking into the medical tent after you used the latrine. I followed you at a remove. They wouldn't let me in to sit with you. I thought I heard your voice. If voices had colors, yours was as gray as the sky. It was the color of the new world. As if a mist of rain had crept into you. Had spoiled you like the earth. You sounded like you were rotting from the roots. I knew you were done. There was no light left in you. Whatever had remained in you when we renewed our vows had been extinguished. I returned to our tent. You were soon to follow, smelling of rubbing alcohol. I asked when the light had gone out. You didn't answer. After a while, I said, it's okay, I'll carry the light for you.

The days didn't grow brighter. Low clouds straggled by, threatening to bury us. At first I thought it was affecting your vision. You began to stumble on your walks to the latrine. Your feet spread a foot apart, your knees and hips locked at joint. You staggered. No one noticed. No one noticed anything anymore. Still, somehow you would make it there and back. Until you didn't. You collapsed in the gravel. Chunks of it tore your cheeks, nested in your forearms, dirtied your clothing. I ran to you. Pulled you into my arms. Wiped away the dust. Pulled the small rocks from your skin. Covered your wounds. It was all I could manage, to lift you, to carry you back to the tent. It was then that I whispered to you that I would keep track of the days. That I would recall everything that you forgot, everything you missed. That I would record our surroundings the way you once did in your journals. But I wouldn't be so meticulous. The way you'd delicately drawn the flora, their data dutifully entered. My drawings are not as lovely as yours. I attempted to draw an MRE. It was lopsided, out of proportion, the light reflecting oddly. It was nothing like your illustration of the apple tree. The delicate valley along the leaf spine where you'd drawn gentle webs of green with your colored pencils. My data is prose. It wanders, gets sidetracked forever, loses itself in subjective digressions, not neatly categorized and tabled like your writing. You said once that I was the heart to your mind. That we were the whole. That we were worthless apart. It struck me as odd that I was meant to be the heart but you were the one who saw beauty in everything. Until violence left your eyes dull and lifeless. You cried when the gangs found your journals. When they piled them in their rucksacks and pulled you into the yard. It was the last time I tried to fight them, raising my body from the floor, just to be kicked and bludgeoned with axe handles. Why they let us live, I'll never understand.

When the gangs infiltrated the camps and we were pushed out, I gathered you in your sheet, careful not to disturb you. You'd grown so thin, I was able to bundle you, tie the sheet behind my neck, carry you as I walked west toward the shore. The thunder came. Endless rolling claps buried in the looming clouds. I feared the rain would come. Poison our skin. Blind us in our last moments. But it did not. The grass broke beneath us. Sometimes when I stopped to rest, it needled through my thinworn slacks. I worried it would prick my skin. Pollute my blood. I saw no one on that walk. For days we journeyed without so much as a shadow. I asked you what you thought sometimes but you never answered. I took to singing to calm my nerves. To pass time. To feel anything besides my legs moving. Mostly I sang the songs you used to ask me to play on guitar during those cold winter nights when we sat by the fire. It makes me nostalgic for a time I've never known, you had said. It makes me nostalgic for a time we had, I said as I rambled over a dry creekbed miles away from the refugee camp. You didn't reply. Perhaps both are true, I whispered.

The weather began to turn, the nights growing longer. I held you in my arms, rocked you until I fell to sleep, shivering and exhausted. We wouldn't last much longer. We wouldn't survive the cold. I wished I could cut myself open, store you in my chest, keep you warm.

Some nights it was all I could do to crank the ham radio. To give it enough life to hear other worlds. Worlds that weren't dying. I listened to a quiz show called *Whose Cough is it?* Contestants listened to audio clips of British celebrities coughing and guessed who it was for cash and prizes. I was surprised to hear that Richard Ayoade had such a robust cough. He was usually so mousey. The game show host reported pollutants from our country had traveled through the atmosphere and had made their way to Isles. This, he said, creates optimal conditions for a hearty cough. I listened to the program until I fell asleep. I thought I had seen a band of stars through a thin layer of clouds, but realized I was slipping into a dream. I awoke the next day to find a seagull struggling to walk next to me. It spread its wings and splayed its feathers. When it couldn't take flight, it pecked at itself, trying desperately to solve the problem. Eventually he gave up, puffed his chest, lay on his feet, and closed his eyes. I'd not seen an animal in so long, I thought I was dreaming. The next morning, I awoke to find it dead. Frost coating its black eyes.

This morning I found myself unable to stand. My legs wouldn't support our weight. They clinched, spasmed, collapsed. It'll be okay, I told you. You didn't reply. The night came on the tail of a cold wind. It whispered in the dead grass. At first, I thought you were trying to speak. I fell asleep again, and when I awoke, I was pleased to discover I had enough strength to crank the radio. I listened to another radio show from England. They played a song from the eighties. I hummed along and rocked you in my arms. The juice began to run out. The radio losing reception and eventually falling silent. A snowflake fell on my nose. Then another. When I held my breath, I thought I could hear the ocean in the distance.

In the Swamp Between the Cities and the Shore, a Girl

This is what the doctor knows. The girl in room seventy-six only refers to herself as the girlfriend. They found her wandering through the Everglades clutching a human metatarsal. The bone covered in dried blood, her face smeared with black mud. Authorities have yet to find a DNA match to the bone or the girl. The doctor sits at his desk and considers the file before him. He searches for any clues as to what may have transpired in the swamp but there are few details in her file save for a few vague testimonies recorded during the initial interviews with the girl calling herself the girlfriend.

He pours a cup of coffee for himself and then a cup of water for the girl calling herself the girlfriend. He cracks the blinds and lets the sunlight come in a smooth slant. He then checks his desk for any sharp objects. Once he is sure he's prepped the room, he buzzes down for the orderlies to escort the girl calling herself the girlfriend to his office.

When she arrives, he finds himself caught off guard for the woman who enters the room looks nothing like the half mad feral woman in the photo in his file on the girl calling herself the girlfriend. There is nothing, in fact, feral about her. Her walk is so graceful, she appears to float over the tiled floor. Her thin wrists cocked in such a way as if she might be preparing to enter the third position in a ballet class. Too is her voice steady and warm. The doctor greets the girl calling herself the girlfriend and she takes a seat as fluidly as she walked. Crossing her left leg over the right, she smiles at the doctor, who offers her a cup of water and introduces himself. Describing the ways in which he envisions their scheduled sessions to run, the doctor keeps his voice level but cheerful, as if promising, without promising, a resolution that satisfies both he and the girl calling herself the girlfriend.

The girl calling herself the girlfriend sips his water, her bottom lip folding over the edge with a subtle grip. Smiling, she uses her pinky to clear the well-combed hair from the periphery of her eye. Of course, she says.

Sitting behind his desk, he asks the girl calling herself the girl-friend where she grew up.

Happyville, Florida, the girl calling herself the girlfriend says.

Surprised that she is so receptive to his line of questioning, he leans in. I've been there, he says, a fine community.

A fine community indeed, she says.

He follows up with a few more distant questions, questions about her family and childhood and receives similar answers that reflect the consensus view of reality. Perhaps, he writes in his notes, she simply needs someone to show a vested interest. Then he begins to ask her about the days leading up to her rescue.

Do you remember how long you'd been in the Everglades? He said.

There grows a look in the girl calling herself the girlfriend's eye that seems to the doctor otherworldly—as if changing color or shape. He writes the word possessed. Why he has chosen the word *possessed*, he can't rightly say but it is his first thought, and he believes, the best thought.

He asks the question again. This time the girl calling herself the girlfriend reacts slightly different. Humming first and then forming her lips around a word she can't quite find, the girl calling herself the girlfriend finally opts to say nothing at all. This seems to be the case with most questions, save for those things, which occurred in the girl calling herself the girlfriend's life before the swamp.

When his session ends, the doctor reviews his notes. He is perplexed by how little she is willing to reveal. At the beginning of the session, he suspected she was hiding things intentionally, so he'd thoroughly explained doctor-patient confidentiality, assuring her that this confidentiality reached beyond legality, that it was a personal code he would never violate, no matter the penalty, that it was an impenetrable blanket of security that ensured a safe place for his patients. This did not seem to gain him any new ground, and whenever he'd brought the subject up again, the girl calling herself the girlfriend would always smile and suggest that she was not capable of misdeeds, especially ones that might require such protection.

He now understands that she is not hiding things, but, rather, there are things hiding inside of her.

As time passes and the doctor becomes more familiar with the girl calling herself the girlfriend, they begin to grow more comfortable in each other's presence. This, he thinks, is the way the matter should progress and he is pleased with the natural ease with which this particular aspect of the therapy is going. Though she never answers how long she'd been in the swamp or how she'd gotten there or how she'd come into possession of the small bone she carried with her, the doctor is able to help her reclaim other memories through indirect questioning. These answers are always incomplete. Though she knows she grew up in Happyville, she left as a child and can't remember the name of the city she lived in after. She did not attend college opting instead to take a job, but she cannot remember exactly what she did only that it involved a metal stapler and a typewriter. Occasionally she says it involved a microscope. Still other times, she believes it was not a microscope but a record player. The stapler, she says, I know for sure.

The doctor's colleagues have competing theories about the girl calling herself the girlfriend. Dr. Jenks, a cognitive specialist, believes she has retrograde amnesia from head trauma. Father McGowan, a wise man with degrees in divinity studies, philosophy, and psychology, believes she suffers from repressed memories surrounding a terrible tragedy that befell her in her youth and can no longer cope. Despite an MRI that indicates otherwise, Dr. Zeil believes there is something physically wrong with the girl calling herself the girlfriend's brain, something dividing her brain and preventing it from functioning properly, something yet unknown to the medical community, and though Dr. Zeil is a renowned neurosurgeon, he simply doesn't have enough evidence to support his request to run further scans. Each of these theories may contain a kernel of truth but the doctor is unwilling to speculate on paper officially until he has made more progress with the girl calling herself the girlfriend.

It isn't long before the director of the hospital begins calling the doctor weekly to check in on the status of the girl calling herself the girlfriend (whom the director unaffectionately refers to as *swamp girl* or *bone lady* or in his less articulate moments *the freebie*) as he wants to clear the bed out for paying patients, ones who aren't staying as a courtesy to local law enforcement. Every time he uses such nicknames, the doctor corrects him by saying it is a matter of professionalism they refer to the patient by her chosen name until such a time they discover her given name and then, as a matter of best practices, they should call her by her given name and discontinue using her chosen name altogether. Each time the director retorts verbatim that it doesn't matter much what he calls her as long as they are making progress, to which the doctor replies that he is hopefully optimistic.

Placing lumps of modeling compound on a table in the back of his office, the doctor looks out his window and onto the yard behind the hospital. Several patients wander along the brick paths between the flower gardens and bushes. He wonders if they ever feel as peaceful as they look among those fuchsia blooms or if they're trapped in a moment of confusion, or worse terror, as some horrifying tragedy returns to fill their bones and cloud their minds. He is nearly touching the glass when the nurse announces the arrival of his patient. Flattening his shirt at the sides where it sometimes bulges, he turns and greets the girl calling herself the girlfriend and asks her to join him at the table by the window.

This, he tells her, is a free expression activity. We will ask one another questions while we sculpt things. The idea is to focus on what we are creating, which takes some of the pressure off what we're saying.

The girl calling herself the girlfriend touches a lump of red compound, lightly as if the slightest movement might provoke it to swallow her into its mass and devour her completely. Pulling it closer, she carefully dents the sides and says, Sure.

Is red your favorite color, the doctor says.

No. It's just the color I selected.

She thinks for a moment, working the compound into a thin strand, rolling it smooth against the table, her eyes focused on the books lining the walls of the office.

Why this career, she asks, mental health?

The doctor recounts his reasons for selecting the profession, telling her that he has always felt a calling to help people. Who, he says, after all, is more underserved than those suffering from mental complications? The girl calling herself the girlfriend seems to accept his answer.

I prefer that phasing, the girl calling herself the girlfriend says, mentally ill sounds so permanent. A sentence, you know?

The doctor agrees, talks about spectrums, about successes, about human resolve.

He keeps his questions light, never once steering into the swamp, the bone, or the amnesia. She seems fascinated by his history and he is happy to share with her an appropriate amount. When she looks away, the doctor glances at her compound. She constructed two small bodies: one yellow, one red. Their thick legs holding them upright, their thin arms threatening to fall away. Their misshapen hands locked together with a fingerprint.

During the middle of a question, the girl calling herself the girlfriend interrupts the doctor; What is your biggest fear, she asks.

With trepidation, the doctor answers, That I will fail those around me. It is a careful answer but contains enough truth that it isn't an outright lie. This is the game, he assures himself, to gain the trust of the patient without being too vulnerable.

She makes a small noise and then offers, I'm scared of being alone. Looking into the sunlight collecting in an oblong space upon the floor, the girl calling herself the girlfriend then separates the hands of the figures. The silence in the room seems to press down upon them.

This must be a very scary time for you then.

Maybe. She turns to the window and pulls a hand off one of the figures and rubs it for an instant on the edge of her bottom lip, lost in thought, before finally slipping it into her mouth and swallowing it. It's hard not to feel alone, she says, when you can't remember who you are.

You're not alone here. You have me, he says, smiling.

I can't decide if I'm stuck with you or you're stuck with me.

The doctor pushes his compound into a circle, forming two eyes and a smile into the surface with the blade of his thumbnail. You're free to go when the evaluation period is over, he says.

Go where, she says.

That's what we want to find out.

When the session ends, the girl calling herself the girlfriend asks if she can take one of the figures to her room. He sees no harm in this and allows it. When she selects the sculpture with the missing hand, the doctor asks if she rather might opt to take the one that doesn't have a missing appendage, but the girl calling herself the girlfriend insists upon taking the one she's already selected. The doctor begins cleaning up the materials as the nurse escorts the girl calling herself the girlfriend down to the community recreation room.

On the next occasion, the doctor, having had such success with art therapy, continues with this method opting this time to use a set of crayons and some paper. They busy themselves drawing, he in red, orange, and green, she in silver, black, blue, and gray, which looks to the doctor nearly identical to the silver. The doctor is no hand at crafts, especially in drawing, specifically with crayons; however, the girl calling herself the girlfriend proves a natural at it. Her lines near perfect, the shading even, her gradients, blending smoothly from black to blue to silver and into the white of the page. Where the doctor chooses to draw the sun, with rays bursting forth in terribly jagged lines, the girl calling herself the girlfriend, chooses to draw a black crescent moon so sharp at the edges it bears an eerie resemblance to a scythe. From that sharp edge, a light radiates upon the Capitoline Wolf. Though upon closer inspection, he sees it's not quite the Capitoline Wolf, for instead of children suckling upon the teats, the girl calling herself the girlfriend has drawn men chewing at the undercarriage, tearing it asunder.

The doctor points to wolf and says, What's its name?

Amber, she says.

Why Amber, he says.

She shrugs and begins drawing a sky filled with shimmering stars. Amply distracted by her celestine sky, the doctor asks her about the name she's chosen for herself.

It's all I can remember, she says, I am the girlfriend of someone. I can't remember who, but he loves me very much.

He must be worried, the doctor says, his voice level and warm, that professional caring smooth he's practiced for so many years.

Probably, she says, but I know his love is always with me.

The doctor asks her what this means but she can only say, I feel it, and very little else. He begins asking her how she'd met the boyfriend. She is able to elaborate on this with remarkable precision though, the doctor admits in his notes, the details seem to surprise her, as if she's pulled them from fragments of a dream. They'd met at a holiday party. They'd traded numbers and began having nightly phone conversations. It seemed, the girl calling herself the girlfriend says, to take a long time to make it to our first date, but I'm glad we waited because we really got to know each other.

I lost him once, she says. Her eyes seem to change colors or shape for a moment, as if another person has slipped inside the shell of her and is looking out at the doctor. The girl calling herself the girlfriend picks up another crayon and smiles, her eyes returning to her. She says, but he came back and he'd never leave again. She holds her picture up, her face aglow with a child-like glee. You should frame it, she jokes.

On another meeting she reveals the boyfriend had been accepted to graduate school and often spent nights in classes, which had given her some concern. She quizzed him on his whereabouts, his female friends he'd met, his car's mileage, what he'd eaten, going so far as to ask him the same questions at different intervals to see if there were any variations in the answers.

I'd become a real pill, she says. It surprises the doctor that the girl calling herself the girlfriend can remember so much about her relationship with her boyfriend and so very little else. She cannot, for example, remember the name of the university he attended, though she can remember it had a tower or pillar or steeple; she cannot remember the boyfriend's name but that she had called him either, dove, lamb, or kitten; she cannot remember what he studied, though she thinks he had many small books, or one large book, or a complicated system of spiral-bound course packets. These inconsistencies sometimes seem to collect upon themselves on days when she is less engaged in her crafts. They multiply and grow more cumbersome as she progresses through the session until she can no longer make it through the story as she becomes too confused and begins crying from frustration or simply shutting down.

Each time the doctor tries to pivot from these productive moments into finding out about what happened in the swamp, he is met by the same opaque wall. The same look. The same lips trying to wrap her mouth around a word. Finding it impossible to progress with the session, the doctor waits until the end of the session to ask questions that might trigger such bewilderment.

Though his colleagues find little worth in art therapy, calling it "touchy-feely" or "expressionistic craft time," the doctor finds his progress with the girl calling herself the girlfriend remarkable and believes he can duplicate the forward progression. However, he finds that the girl calling herself the girlfriend creates the exact same art objects and speaks about the same things. Even when he attempts to steer her, she bends her way back to the original subject. There is one exception. On the occasions where they work with the modeling compound, she will point to the red body, the one on her left and say, this, this is not it. This is not the original. When the doctor asks her what she means, she shrugs and says, I don't know. It just isn't.

Moving forward, the doctor introduces new activities, to unearth new results. He understands the girl sitting before him is a complicated puzzle like nothing he's ever seen. Before long, he finds himself obsessed, refusing new patients and meeting with the girl calling herself the girlfriend on a daily basis—challenging himself to keep her receptive to decoding as long as he can before she reaches the threshold of her communicative potential.

A few months into the treatment, the doctor is called out of town to attend a funeral of a childhood friend. Though stricken with sadness at the loss, he can't help himself from missing his daily sessions with the girl calling herself the girlfriend. What had happened to her car, her phone, her shoes? What is it that called her back to the shadows, those prehistoric waterways standing in opposition to the gleaming bright modern cities along the coastlines? He thinks back to his departed friend, to their hijinks in the forest beyond the neighborhoods, how they escaped the confines of the man-made world to return to some primitive time where boys ran the world in wild packs, screaming and naked beneath the trees. But, for the girl calling herself the girlfriend, he can't say. Perhaps it was a wrong turn, a late return after a day of nature hiking gone awry, or a flat tire. Or perhaps she went there to return to her primal self, to run wild like the wolf among the cypress and orchid and got carrieed away.

The day after the funeral, the doctor calls the director of the hospital to assuage his concerns regarding the doctor's diminished workload and reports that he is making a great deal of progress with the girl calling herself the girlfriend and thanks the director for allowing him to focus on the patient as a matter of expedience. The director, somewhat perturbed by the matter, replies curtly that it's in the best interest of the hospital for the doctor to return to his usual duties as soon as possible.

When the doctor returns to work, the girl calling herself the girlfriend doesn't feel well so the doctor agrees to meet in her room. She lies there prostrate on her bed, her skin pale.

I thought you'd abandoned me, she says, her voice thin inside her like a tiny bird caught in the cage of her chest.

He tells her about the funeral and her lips pull across her teeth in a kind of smile and she whispers that she'll let it slide this time.

She has no fever, no discernable ailment the doctor can identify, but she still exhibits the physical signs of someone suffering from a severe viral infection. At first the doctor worries she'd contracted an illness in the swamp. That something was growing inside of her, a wormlike parasite curling inside her intestines or brain. He runs a battery of tests with the medical team but the results are negative.

They sit in her room that evening, she on the bed, the sheet bundled at her feet, he on an old wooden chair. Though the doctor rarely visits patients' rooms, it seems as if hers is more sparsely decorated than the others. There are no photographs torn from the magazines they provide their patients, no family photos, no excess artwork at all. Her only decoration is the sculpture she'd crafted during their session, and even that has been reduced to little if anything at all. The head, the legs, one of the arms, all gone.

What happened to your sculpture, the doctor says.

Without a glance toward it, she says, I don't remember.

This concerns the doctor. If she is losing new memories, her trauma could, despite the negative result on the CT scans, be something more problematic. He begins asking questions about things they've discussed previously. With weakened voice and slow response, she answers each correctly. Lifting her head from her pillow a little, she asks if she can sleep awhile. When the doctor stands to leave, scooting the chair back several inches with his calves, the girl calling herself the girlfriend asks, in a panicked breath, if he might stay a while longer, that his presence comforts her. He nods and eases back into his chair.

The gentle rhythm of her chest rising and falling so slightly as to be practically impossible. He feels an odd compulsion to cradle her in his arms as if she is his own child. Instead, he pulls the covers up to her neck and sits back in his chair, lolling off to sleep until one of the nurses steps in for the girl calling herself the girlfriend's nightly check in. She, surprised to see the doctor, drops her clipboard but manages to catch it against her thigh. Whispering, *sorry*, he steps around her, taking one last look at the dismembered sculpture on the dresser, noticing the fine undulating ridges from the ragged backs of her teeth.

—

The director calls the doctor moments after he's arrived and started his first cup of coffee. He inquires about the status of the girl calling herself the girlfriend so he can report back to the board in an afternoon meeting. The doctor promises a diagnosis as well as a hypothesis as to the circumstances that led her to the swamp. He asks the director for another month. Again, the director answers with a lack of enthusiasm, Your reputation can only buy you a limited amount of time. Any other doctor would have been rejected upon the first proposal of a reduced patient load. The doctor thanks the director and prepares his office for his session with the girl calling herself the girlfriend.

The doctor places new modeling compound upon the table. He asks the same questions he's asked before. The girl calling herself the girlfriend answers with the exact answers she had previously, no embellishments no fluctuations. This time, however, she does not shape things out of the compound.

Don't you want to shape things, the doctor says.

No, the girl calling herself the girlfriend says. We've done this enough.

Yes, but I thought you might want to make another one. To replace the one that's been damaged.

No, the girl calling herself the girlfriend says, I don't need it.

But wouldn't you like a new one?

He's fine, she says.

I didn't know it was a he.

Of course it's a he. You can see it's a man. It's evident.

I'm an old man, my eyes not what they used to be. Please let me know what I'm missing.

The color for one. Red is a masculine color. It's the color of passion.

The doctor points out that he has plenty of red clay and that she is more than welcome to use any of it she wants. The girl calling herself the girlfriend shows no interest. When the doctor persists, she replies that there can only be one of any thing. The doctor asks the girl calling herself the girlfriend if she can retrieve the sculpture from her room and she complies.

They sit there for a moment, the daylight cool through the windows, resting in odd places between the wall and floor, the sculpture lopsided upon the desk. As she sat there, rubbing her finger over the disfigured figure, she does not look like the frail woman who called him to her bedside. She is composed and strong like she had been at their first meeting, the body of a ballet dancer, a back hewn of oak with a purl of muscles along her calves barely hidden by skin. Pushing a trashcan with his foot, the doctor asks the girl calling herself the girlfriend to toss the sculpture inside. As he suspects, she refuses. He gives it a moment and then stands as if to take the sculpture. She, swift as cobra, snatches it and forces the sculpture into her mouth. Though, not all of it. A very slender piece she cuts free with her lips and attempts to stow between her fingers. This, the doctor allows for he has his answer. Something strange fills him, coldness in his head and warmth around his chest.

He writes as she chews the hardened mass of modeling compound. Then, upon reading his notes, he regards the girl calling herself the girlfriend. She looks smaller than normal as if reduced, bent in the chair trying to keep the last piece of her sculpture hidden from him. He grins, an attempt to ease her worries and then dismisses her, thanking her for her coming in. The nurse comes to escort the girl calling herself the girlfriend to her room. She stands and walks, reluctance in each step. Before she's completely out of the office, the girl calling herself the girlfriend turns and asks, Will I see you again?

The doctor nods and says, Of course.

That night he receives a call from the director of the hospital for an update on the case, citing once again that it is unprecedented, even for a man of his caliber, to take so much time from his case load to focus on one patient, continuing on to say that the board decided to release the girl calling herself the girlfriend to the authoraites. Yes, the doctor says, I understand. I will have a full diagnosis by the morning.

Closing his file, he considers the options. It is a matter of time before the girl calling herself the girlfriend remembers the unspeakable thing that happened in the swamp. If he tells her the outcome of his study, it will undoubtedly hasten her realization. How long would his silence buy her? A month? Two? He does not sleep that night, does not leave the office, instead he researches the missing persons database for men between the ages of twenty-five and thirty who fit the vague descriptions the girl calling herself the girlfriend shared during their meetings. Thousands of names sifted down through the hours to a handful. Refining through the darkling hours of night until he is left with one name. From there he is able to trace the girl calling herself the girlfriend through social media.

Daylight seeps up through the horizon as he types his report.

On the evening of, he begins, working through the events, *Amber Sims drove her boyfriend, Shaw Roberts, into the Everglades.* Before he finishes the sentence, he pauses, thinking of the girl calling herself the girl-friend, the girl who he will never see as Amber, no matter how many photographs or official records he sees confirming the name. Isn't it possible, after all, that she's become an entirely different person through the mysterious chemistry of the mind? How delicately she'd handled her crafts, how sweet she'd been to the staff and to the doctor himself. Perhaps, he reasons, she is no longer Amber at all but has transitioned into the girlfriend. He types, *alligator, trauma*. He stares at these words for a while. His fingers over the delete key.

The sun rises above the tree line, its light cruel and unforgiving. The doctor hits send on the email containing his report. He steps away from the desk, notes in his hand. He makes himself some coffee as he has a long day ahead of him. He sips it, finding it more bitter than ever before; he inserts his notes into the paper feed on his document shredder. Clicking the machine on, he listens to the motor for a second, reconsidering his decision, then nudges the pages toward the mouth. As he walks away toward the bathroom, he can hear the faint whirl of the blades chewing at the paper. A month, he thinks, or two. It's better than nothing. It's better than nothing.

After the Ossuary

1.

They had planned the trip to Prague after the miscarriage. It was Kent's way of giving them a vacation to look forward to during those bleak winter months when it felt as if the world was incapable of producing new life. For the most part, the trip was off to a good start, and when complications did arise, Margot and Kent were quick to make the best of things. When the flight was less lavish than they'd anticipated, they got drunk on wine and managed to sleep in the cramped seats of the jet without interruption; though they missed their connecting flight, they stayed in Berlin for a few days, eating Saharan falafel along the shady banks of the canals; and though the air-conditioning in their Air B&B was broken, they took day naps on the balcony, drank white wine spritzers, and embarked on short walking stints, taking in the majestic architecture of the town.

It seemed at first the tensions that had arisen after the loss of their child had completely evaporated, but as the temperatures continued to rise in Prague, Margot began to feel them reconstitute and seep to the surface, beneath the sweat that haunted their bodies. Still they were able to keep their frustrations at bay until they took their first day trip. Kent had caught wind of a church in the country decorated in human bones and was beside himself with excitement.

Kuntá Hora, he said, a boyish excitement edging his voice, it's listed as one of the things tourists absolutely need to see while in Prague.

A church of bones, Margot said, that's your idea of a vacation.

Absolutely need to see, Kent said, splaying his hands out like a showman when he stressed *need*.

We can still see the castle and eat sausage while we're here though, right?

The very next day, he assured her.

Margot and Kent arrived at the Praha Hlavni Nadrazi with plenty of time to spare. Margot craved an egg sandwich, so despite their wishes to eat only local cuisines, they grabbed breakfast at an American fast-food chain and ate in silence as the ceiling speakers showered them in hits from the eighties.

Look at the sign, Margot said, Does it seem weird they haven't listed our train yet?

The man said it wouldn't show until twenty minutes before we leave.

That's so weird, isn't it?

Like I said…

Yeah, Europe's different. Margot took a bite from her sandwich and hummed to "Love Like Blood."

They'd never play this in the States, Kent said.

Margot shrugged. She shrugged a lot at the things Kent said. With ten years on her, he'd traveled the world a good many times and seemed to know a little about everything, which he was always in the mood to share if anyone would listen. She chose to find it endearing most of the time, but sometimes, she found it, well, shrug-worthy.

When it was twenty minutes to departure and they still hadn't seen their train listed, Margot looked at Kent and said, Well?

He walked around the screens and looked at the back (though they both knew there was nothing there) then took in the amassing crowd for a moment in dumb silence and said, I'm not sure. Let's find the ticket booth.

Following Kent through the train station for ten minutes, a strangepulse of annoyance resurrected in Margot's neck, a funny thrush of blood only Kent seemed to bring about. After a while, she stood there and let him wander, seemingly unaware he was alone. He'd come back to the screen, stare at it with his eyes wide and then come to the conclusion, as she had some time ago, their train wasn't going to be listed. Were they at the wrong station? Would they make the train? Kent didn't seem to know the answers.

Eventually he left, only to return, red-faced, and say, I found the ticket booth. It was down two floors.

We missed our train, Margot said, looking not at Kent, but at an elderly woman playing "Rodrigo" on a public piano.

Yes.

I thought you were the expert, Margot said, then added, I'm sorry. I'm just frustrated. I understand, Kent said, rubbing her back. The woman down there wasn't very helpful.

So, we don't go?

We can still go, I just wanted to check if it's cool that we buy tickets for a later train.

It sometimes bothered her that a grown man still used the word *cool*, but Margot said nothing, just nodded and Kent vanished again into the maddening rush of travelers.

A small child and his mother walked into a grocery store and Margot found herself following them and smiling as the mother pointed to things and spoke to her child in Czech. For some time, she trailed behind them, stepping closer each time they stopped. It wasn't an impulse with which she was familiar, and when it dawned on her she was watching them, perhaps a little too closely, she changed direction and lost herself in the aisles, until she found some distraction in the various foodstuffs stacked around her. The cheese and meats were fresh, sandwiches wrapped daily with locally baked breads, the candy aisle was small but colorful, bursting with pastel wrappers and golden foil, and a vast menagerie of confectionary treats lined the bakery counter, each option more tantalizing than the last. Everything seemed healthier, the ingredient lists smaller, and if she could've read Czech, she had no doubts she'd find the ingredients to be all-natural.

How lovely to have a grocery store in the train station, where commuters could pick up dinner on their way home from work. Margot tried to imagine the HyVee in the local greyhound station back home, the crackheads and homeless stumbling through the aisles touching the bread. But the grocery stores back home were so much bigger, the chip aisles infinite and health food limited. She favored the small shops in Europe. The need to go to specialty stores. The socializing inherent in a day's shopping. It all felt so personal. Everything back home seemed focused on convenience, but in Europe, she and Kent were putting in ten thousand steps on a bad day and meeting more people.

Perhaps she could suggest they walk more when they got home? Frequent more of the boutique shops around town. This thought pleased her. The two of them carrying their bags from store to store, walking along the roads in the summer sun. A baby strapped to her chest.

But there was no baby—and when she thought of one, there

in the aisles of the store, she only saw a small bloody corpse, Kent slipping sunglasses on it, saying, *Look who's cool now*!

As if on cue, Kent's voice broke her thoughts. When you vanished, I panicked a little. Margot didn't reply. He said, Are you okay? You're just staring into space.

What could she tell him? When she thought of a child, it was always dead? That she had dreams of a baby crying in the house? She touched a candy bar and said, Everything here tastes better.

Local and less preservatives, Kent said, picking up a package of cheese. I don't even think they factory farm. He stopped when Margot shook her head and taunted, Mer mer mer mer mer.

I'm mansplaining again, sorry.

Can you mansplain the ticket situation to me now?

Train tickets are good for the day, so if a person misses their train, they can catch the next one.

What if a lot of people miss their trains?

I don't know.

Do you think they have to kick people off?

I doubt it. Let's not worry about it and just get on the train and see.

Margot chewed on the inside of her lip for a moment and said, Do you know where we're going this time?

Kent pulled a map from his pocket and pointed to a section the man had circled for him. That's our platform.

2.

When they arrived to Kutná Hora, they hurried along the winding streets of the town to see Sedec Ossuary, where Kent wandered among the bones and took photographs and Margot sat on a ledge beneath a towering stack of femurs where the sun slanted in through the murky air. She thought of the old blind monk gathering the bones of the dead, stacking them in his permanent dark. Building the chandelier of spines, the arch of skulls, the alien wickerwork of boney wall patterns. Did it seem so macabre to him or did his blindness conceal the horrors that the sighted experience when confronted with their mortality? Certainly, it was not lost on him. And the smell, she wondered, was that mildew gathering in the furthest recesses of the stacks of bones or was that the smell of death, damp and dull? Where Kent found a childlike glee in such abjection, Margot couldn't quite put her finger on her feelings. It was a quiet kind of terror collecting in the pockets of her spine. A slinky kind of shadow.

She needed a beer. It wasn't necessarily thirst working up inside Margot as much as it was a deep desire to feel lighter. Death seemed to weigh inside her. Walking out of the cemetery, she asked Kent to wait while she grabbed a drink from a vendor across the way, but Kent, who wanted a cold soda, suggested they visit an old bar they'd passed earlier. They walked for some time before they came upon it, doors locked, shades drawn.

Without a word, Margot pivoted and they continued toward the train station in silence. As a boy with a backpack passed them, he raised his head and said something. Was it a greeting or a curse? It had the soft sound of a familiar greeting, but certainly the boy was old enough (perhaps nine or ten) to mark tourists from a great distance. Margot's womb quivered and she stopped dead for a moment.

What is it? Kent asked.

She looked over her shoulder at the boy. He turned around,

walking backwards, and parted his tan lips to release a thin white smile. Was he mocking her?

Nothing, she said and walked on.

Why'd we stop then?

Are there Gypsies here?

I think that's racist.

You think it is?

I don't know, Kent said, a rare look of confusion pushing his brow into waves.

Popping her lips together, that thing she did when she found herself short of language, she looked at her phone and said, I want to get to the train early so we have a seat.

Okay.

And I want that beer.

As they neared the station, Kent stopped to bleat at a few goats feeding along the edge of a yard. The train station, a barebones kind of place, sat in the distance, across the street from a dismal looking Asian restaurant, so she continued walking without Kent. She wasn't going to stop until she got a beer.

She bought a pilsner and a chocolate wafer from the convenience shop and descended the cross-over steps to the platform. An artist had painted a colorful town map but all Margot could think about in the unlit tunnel were the thousands of unmarked bodies stacked atop one another in the Sedlec Ossuary. People lined up at the exit to buy pins and stickers and mugs. A tourist trap built on the tragic death of the sick. Again, something cold and foreign, a ghostly bone scraping, moved inside of her. How many children had died in the plague? Why were their bones hidden? She began stroking her stomach the way she had when she was pregnant. So familiar it was, so comforting. But then, she remembered the pains, the blood, the hospital stay, and dropped her hands to her sides, quickened her pace, took the steps up two at a time until she stood on the platform winded and hot.

The train was delayed, and because of this a glut of commuters packed the platform. When it finally arrived, the crowd lunged forward in a wave, pressing Kent and Margot into a first-class car. Kent pushed along the hallway, fighting for a chance at seats in second-class, but was jammed up next to the water closet. There, in the heat of the others, they stood, sweating as the train rolled on. Whatever cold feeling had worked itself inside her in the tunnel was replaced by the heat of a near asphyxiating claustrophobia.

Holding onto the door handle, Kent blocked the window and, if Margot could have managed to get a word through the panic building inside her, she'd have asked him to trade places. Instead she hugged against his back and attempted to calm her ragged breath. Her knees were getting weak and she began to worry about getting trampled if she fell. Everything seemed to be pressing in on her, and just as she contemplated screaming to expand her lungs, the train stopped and several people hopped off, leaving the two of them alone in the vestibule.

Let's go in there, he said, pointing into first class, it's air-conditioned.

I don't want to get yelled at by the ticket guy, Margot said.

I'll handle it.

He opened the door and Margot followed him.

When they arrived back in Prague, they went to a Medieval restaurant across the street from Old Town Hall. They descended a spiral staircase lined with taxidermized animals. Squirrels, bear cubs, and foxes stared through the gloom, their glassy eyes cold.

A host greeted them and said, Welcome to China.

Though it seemed a funny greeting, she smiled and said, Thank you.

In the back of the bunker, A Czech folk band played a mix of traditional songs and show tunes. As they launched into "Habanera" the other tourists began to sing along in a trance-like moan.

I get it now, Kent said.

Margot kept her eyes on the menu. You get what?

China.

China? Margot asked.

Kent tapped on the edge of the laminated menu and she followed his hand to see that they were surrounded by scores of Chinese tourists.

We should leave.

Oh, he didn't mean anything by it.

He meant everything by it, Kent.

It's not like he called them names. He was just, you know, warning us.

A hot thread of anger ran along her neck as she lowered her chin and refocused on the menu so she didn't have to look at the hundreds of dead animals lining the walls. When she finally met Kent's eyes, they were filled with abject zeal. Kent's eyes never seemed to get bloodshot because he never seemed to get tired. She, on the other hand, woke up tired and trudged through the days, working two jobs, in an endless fog.

It was nice Kent paid for things like the trip, but even his generosity had begun to worm itself under her skin after the miscarriage.

Isn't this place great? Kent asked.

She wanted to say no, say that it was another place filled with death he'd talked her into without thinking about the toll it might take on her. Another day he didn't think about the baby.

Sure, she said, choking it all down. Keeping measured. The way her parents had taught her.

She took her time eating her dumplings as Kent stood to snap photos with his vintage camera. He was happy and it tore her up that she couldn't find joy in that. But this was the way it had always been. Maybe it was that he came from money, but things didn't seem to get to him. Only once had she seen his mood completely change. They'd been arguing over moving in together and Kent had made a joke. This was what he always did. Made jokes in uncomfortable situations as a way of coping with them. On good days he was funny, but on the bad days, he was tone deaf, his jokes soulless. When Margot didn't laugh and told him she'd find someone else to live with, someone who actually wanted her around, Kent called her a bitch. She'd felt her stomach lurch and shouted, Maybe your first wife left you because you're a fucking child. Kent shut down for days, barely spoke. About a week later, he told her that his ex-wife had only married him for money. That she'd stolen from his family and left him when he'd confronted her about it.

I was never the same, he had told Margot. You're the first person I've trusted since.

Kent put his hand on her shoulder as he watched the folk band and some hard thing in her heart softened. Margot stroked Kent's leg. He winked at her and then returned to the business of taking photos of the dead.

—

3.

The days grew hotter the longer they stayed. Large orange trucks rolled along the cobblestone streets spraying water into the air. People, needing a break from the heat, ran behind them and showered in the cool mists. As they walked around the city, Margot found herself possessed by the notion that rather than sweating, her body had taken to sloughing away gelatinous layers of skin. Though she knew better, she'd more than once checked her underwear, equally disappointed and grateful to find sweat.

In an attempt to avoid the heat, they left early one morning to hike to Prague Castle, which loomed over the city like a shimmering white star. The first half of the journey was quite pleasant, as Kent indulged Margot's request to stay and watch the Palace Garden peacocks.

When she was a young, Margot had gone to a summer camp for children with working parents—a cheap sleepaway camp in the woods bordering a country club. She would spend the days dodging activities like tie-dying shirts and weaving friendship bracelets to wander through the woods and lure the country club's peacocks away from the greens, where she would sit with them and watch as old white men threw tantrums on the rough in the distance. It was her sanctuary at that horrible camp where the other kids bullied her and called her names and where the wolf spiders seemed to stalk her in the cabin, biting her when she wasn't looking.

When a white peacock emerged between two hedges, she stopped, her breath blocking any words. She had never seen one before and all she could seem to do was sit on the gravel and stare in daft bewilderment until it approached her and then she began to whisper in a special language she'd once shared with the peacocks of her youth.

A toddler in a pair of oversized denim overalls trotted in front of Margot and tossed a small stone at the bird. Grabbing the child's arm, Margot chided her. No, you never hurt animals!

The mother swooped in, pulled her daughter into her arms, and yelled, Don't you touch my child. The toddler cried, a piercing shriek that sent the peacocks running.

Kent attempted to make peace, but Margot stormed out of the gardens and began the long high climb to the castle.

Kent called after her and Margot turned around and shout -ed, What?

What do you mean, what? Back there, what the hell were you thinking?

Fuck that kid.

Kent wanted to laugh and she could see that, but he was doing his best not to. Yeah, fuck that kid. She grabbed his hand but then he said, Baby, you can't just grab a stranger's kid, and she let it go.

That little shit threw a rock at a bird.

I know, but what if that was our….Kent trailed off. The world seemed to press against the back of Margot's eyes. Her breath roiled in her throat. Closing her eyes, she swallowed hard against it. What I mean, is we want to be parents. We need to start acting… Again, Kent trailed off, unable to find the right words.

Margot turned around and began walking again.

Come on, talk to me. Kent said, trailing her.

I told you about the peacocks I used to feed when I was at camp. Kent jogged to catch up and walk by her side. What I didn't tell you is I saw them die.

You saw them die?

I was out there once when hail as big as golf balls started rain- ing down. I tried to help them, but it hurt too much. Margot paused and caught her breath for a moment. From there, I watched as it beat them to death, broke their wings, their spines, cracked their skulls. They tried to get to me. They tried but they just couldn't make it. Some nights I still dream about them out there stumbling around and crying.

Kent took her hand and they walked for some time without speaking. This was the kindest thing he'd done for her in weeks, let her speak, without offering advice. Without trying to calm her by explaining the big life lesson she might glean from her experiences.

The further they climbed, the hotter it seemed to get, until, once again, Margot was overtaken by the feeling she was sloughing away layers of slime that collected in her underwear. She'd scarcely felt so unclean in her life. To make matters worse, she was beginning to chafe, her inner thighs painfully scraping together in the shadows of her denim shorts. Spreading her gait slightly, she hoped to find some relief, but only managed to look strange in her off-balance lumber.

The street curled before them in strange kinks, stepping forever upward in an unsubtle incline—neither steep nor gentle. Never did the castle or its massive cathedral reveal itself to them; instead, the rocky walls, hills, and businesses with their stony dark faces loomed over them so that, when they emerged in a small-town square, they were confused as to which road to take. White directional signs pointed in all directions and more than one seemed to promise a castle. Kent said that they should follow the crowd and so they did.

A group of schoolchildren gathered around them. Kent joked with them and started giving them hi-fives. He was the social one in the relationship. Where he found ease in meeting new people, Margot prickled with anxiety and nausea. She began to put some distance between she and Kent and the children. It was only a few feet, but it was enough.

The climb became steep and Margot bore the full weight of the summer sun. The blood gathered in her cheeks in that way she hated, in the way that looked like she was cold but was not. Her hair clung to her shiny forehead and her breath now came in swift shots, less of it with every step. Had she grown so lazy a leisurely climb made her struggle so? Kent suggested they slow and get a flavored ice from a street vendor who lurked upon the landing. How could he know this would drive her harder to complete the walk? She shook her head, the tip-taps of sweaty hair beating against her skin, and continued on. Kent struggled behind her as well, his cheeks puffed out, his hair shining wet beneath the dazzling sun. There came in her a desire to win. Win what she wasn't sure, but she began to step quicker. They passed families drinking water, sucking on ice, babies crying in harnesses, and the farther they went, the more people they encountered until the stairway was congested with struggling travelers.

Along the final bend, there was a majestic view of Prague, but Margot didn't stop—instead, she found new vigor and strode into the cobblestone opening, where a score of people danced wildly in the spray of a water truck. Kent jogged over and began dancing with strangers below the fountain. He waved for Margot to join, but she stood in the sun, arms crossed. As the children caught up, they too ran into the shower and began giving Kent hi-fives again. It was always so easy for him. He never cared about looking foolish.

Margot made her way to the long line at the gates of the palace. When Kent joined her, dripping wet, they didn't speak. Kent pulled on his shirt to fan his body and made some attempts at starting a conversation but Margot remained silent, annoyed by the sucking of the wet cotton as it came away from his body. The statues above the gates loomed above them, their hands splayed above them as if even they were seeking shelter from the sun.

When they finally made it inside the grounds, Kent said, We need a drink.

Though she wanted only to see the castle and cathedral and return to the city, she capitulated and they went to a café, where they sat in a sunny corner and drank in silence as an American family next to them scrambled to pay a bill after they discovered the café didn't accept cards. The father looked at his wallet as if there might be some pocket he'd forgotten that held a wealth of koruna. Shaking her head, his wife finally turned her back on the man and asked if they'd accept US currency. An agreement was reached as the father slipped his wallet back into his pocket, a broken look in his eyes.

Kent stared beyond the hillside, oblivious as he so often was. Time passed and when it became clear to Margot that Kent wasn't going to ask for a check anytime soon, a pinprick came to her heart. Her eyes narrowed, teeth went to edge, and she hailed a waitress.

People don't do that here, Kent said without taking his eyes off the window.

I don't care. I'm ready to leave.

Cool.

The mother at the next table and said, So cool.

She chided her son for getting chocolate on his shirt. The boy, next to his father, shared the same shameful dumb expression on his face. Margot turned to Kent sitting with his jaw slack, mouth agape slightly. She touched her stomach and wondered if her child would have told jokes at the wrong times, if it would have slept with its mouth agape, snoring, if it would have left the bathroom door open when it took a shit.

4.

I'm sorry, Kent said.

Jesus, Kent, it's all I wanted to do today.

How was I supposed to know they'd close early?

You're the one who acts like he knows every-fucking-thing about Europe. I don't know, maybe look shit up?

Kent stared at a ghoul mask in the window of a curiosity shop. It was a sickly faded kind of chartreuse that, under the blacklight, glowed in an otherworldly haze that seemed to draw attention to the inhuman texture of the cheap latex. Even with the light from the street pouring in through the window, the shadows within eyes, mouth, nose, and wrinkles along the temples were an ethereal black. Sticking from the blunt nose was a long, curving wart that wiggled when the mask turned on its motorized stand. It was, simply put, an unsightly mess, even for a ghoul. Kent didn't speak for a long time, then said, When I was a kid, I wasn't allowed to go trick 'r' treating with my friends. It's kind of all I ever wanted to do. Maybe it's because they forbid it, or maybe I was just naturally attracted to dark shit, I don't know, but I knew my parents wouldn't let me buy this werewolf mask I really wanted. One day I snuck to the comic book store, bought it, hid it under my bed, and made plans with my friends to sneak out on Halloween. It didn't take long for the maid to find it and rat me out; my parents shipped me away to a Baptist retreat that weekend and I missed everything.

Kent went silent again, his finger on the glass, a mischievous thin smile on his face.

Nice story, Margot said, her voice a blade, I'm hungry and annoyed, so what's your point?

Kent winked, opened the door to the curiosity shop, and said, There's always time to set things right.

Walking away, Margot chewed at the inside of her mouth and stepped into the throng of tourists streaming by. The evening was cooler but the dampness was not gone from her. She wanted a beer and a sausage and a goddamned place to sit that wasn't covered in bird shit or urine. Abandoning the push of the crowd, she came upon a small dark road where, beneath a broken streetlamp, glowed an old vendor's cart, and just above it the dim red glow from the vendor's cigarette. As she grew closer, his face emerged from the patchwork of shadows, a dull, tan thing with a dingy white beard. His flat cap obscured his eyes, but when he lifted his head, they came to life in a brilliant sparkle.

Sausage? he asked, a smile revealing a startling white set of teeth.

Please. Do you have beer?

This is Prague, Miss. We all have beer.

Margot laughed and handed the man a fistful of money.

This is too much, miss.

How about you keep the beer coming until it's all gone?

He pulled a few coins from the mess and said, This will do.

The vendor offered his stool and she sat and ate her sausage. Sucking the first beer down, she tried to hand the man more money, but he refused and handed her another pilsner. She knew beer was cheap in Prague, but the math didn't seem right, so she tried again, managing in-between chews to utter, take.

Shaking his head, the man said, This Bud's for you.

Though it wasn't Budweiser, she understood the reference as an act of kindness. She took a swig, a different variety, slightly hoppier, and certainly more potent. After two more, the world began to grow softer around the edges. She was buzzed.

Maybe this was enough, enjoying the silence of a weathered sausage vendor in a dark alley, buzzed and free. Just a few moments to clear her mind. To chase away the disappointment of the day.

A long silhouette emerged in the mouth of the cobblestone street, a specter among the tall buildings. The gait familiar but not the shape. As it grew closer, Margot made out the faint glow of the latex ghoul mask that haunted the window. Easing a baton from his pocket, the vendor stepped forward.

Margot, is that you? Kent said, his voice muffled by the childish mask.

This fool's with me, Margot told the vendor.

He laughed and collapsed the baton back into his pocket.

You shouldn't be walking around dark streets without me.

Before taking another bite from her sausage, she said, Because you're the Europe guy?

Stopping in his tracks, Kent cocked his head sideways like a puppy that didn't understand.

Sizing up the vendor, Kent said, Let's go, Margot.

I'm not finished.

Let's get real food.

Something shifted in her, dropped inside her heart. Her pulse seemed to bounce in her throat, but she didn't reply, only took a last big bite and walked to him.

The old man sat back down and said, Treat her better, man.

Turning on his heel, Kent said, Mind your fucking business.

No. Margot said.

No what? Kent asked.

Apologize to the man.

Kent stared at her, the mask concealing his expression.

Is this about the castle?

No. Apologize.

Kent mumbled an apology to the vendor as Margot stormed off. The awkward trot of Kent behind her ricocheted against the buildings, stopping when he tripped over something metal. As he caught up with her, he lifted the mask somewhat so he could see.

Take off the mask, Kent.

He slipped it back over his face, hobbled around her, and grunted. The Czech Ghoul says we can try tomorrow. We can see the castle and we can eat sausage.

Cut it out.

Grunting and hopping around, Kent took to swinging his arms wildly. A group of tourists stopped and gathered to watch. Raising his arms and spinning, Kent yelled, The Czech Ghoul promises you will get to do everything again. There is always hope. He faced his new audience and said, There is hope for everyone.

The crowd applauded, and though Margot attempted to duck away, the world spun wildly around her, so she stopped and Kent pulled her into a powerful hug. She couldn't see his face, but she knew beneath the foul sagging skin of the mask, he was smiling. Everything seemed wrong. The face too long, his embrace too tight. The crowd still watching and moving in waves. Her legs flimsy and close to giving. Then, in that moment, a rush of blood seemed to flood her, a swarm of heat and a flash of white, and she heard herself yell, But there is no hope. There's no hope for us. There's no hope we'll get back to normal.

His grip on Margot loosened.

What are you talking about, Margot?

I'm talking about us. About this trip. You act like everything is okay. But it's not. We lost our baby, Kent. And you're dancing around in the street like an asshole, and we lost our baby and noth-ing, fucking *nothing*, is going to be okay.

There in the mouth of the side street, the pale light sucking the color from their skin, they regarded one another. Some people in the crowd began to walk away, others chittered and stared in antic-ipation. Kent hovered there, the mask comically long, the mouth agape as if it too had heard her.

Kent, Margot said, but he turned, his hands stuffed in the small tight pockets of his jean shorts, and walked away, back toward their loft. Waiting for a moment, trying desperately to shake the drunk out of her head, she steadied herself. When the ground felt whole again, she stepped forward to follow, but Kent was lost in the throng of tourists.

Though they'd walked between the square and the loft several times, it was much more difficult getting back drunk and alone. She was lousy at navigating on a good day, but drunk and upset, she was useless. The curving streets wrapped endlessly into themselves and she wondered if she wasn't going to end up in some cul-de-sac where, through some dark eastern European miracle, all avenues of escape would vanish leaving her surrounded by marionette shops and banks. The streams of tourists derouted her, forced her into strange viaducts, tunnels, and boulevards. Eventually, with the help of a police officer, she made her way back, but Kent was asleep on the couch, the mask still on his face. She crawled into bed and rode the tail end of her buzz into a long dreamless sleep.

5.

She woke to find Kent in the kitchen, sucking down a protein shake through a straw crudely pushed through the breathing hole of his mask. The sight of him slurping that green milk in the mask, his bare belly protruding slightly above his tighty-whities, was too much. She burst into a laughter. Kent accidentally pulled the straw from the cup when he turned toward her and stood there in his underwear, the shake dripping everywhere. The ghoul mask somehow looking shameful in the daylight. So badly did she want to confront him about the previous night, but not there. Not then. He was too pathetic. She thought of him with their son, if the child had survived. Passing these things onto the boy. Both of them standing in the kitchen, nothing but underwear and Halloween masks on. She shuddered and went to take a shower.

When she was dressed and ready, Kent had left. She waited for a while, but she realized he wasn't coming back, and went to a bar around the corner where she could get dumplings and beer. Her intention was to eat and go to the castle but she never made it. Instead, she spent the better part of the day in the dark pub talking to strangers who seemed all too eager to buy her drinks and swap stories. Emerging from the dank basement, she found herself stumbling home in the honey thick heat.

The days went by like this. Margot waking to find Kent drinking a smoothie in his mask and underwear and return home to him sleeping on the couch. More than once she tried to engage him in conversation but found him unresponsive. One night, when she came home after watching the local ballet company perform, she approached him carefully, stepping forward only when he inhaled deeply, his breath whistling in the slit of the mask, until she was kneeling next to him. The smell of mildew gathering in the mask and the onion-like smell of his body odor was overwhelming. It was clear to her that he wasn't bathing. Wasn't removing the mask even when alone. She thought of him wandering the streets with it on. People staring. People pointing. People giving him money when he stopped to rest like he was a busker. A car alarm rang out in the distance and Kent woke and shook with startle. She tried to speak, to apologize, but he didn't listen; instead, he dressed and walked out of the loft.

Two days passed and there was no sign of him. She called his parents, her mother, their closest friends but no one had heard from Kent. Revisiting some of the places they'd seen, she searched for him. She also visited the torture museum, the Kafka museum, and a creepy puppet theater in hopes of finding him, but came each time to the same result, Kent was gone. When the airline informed her that he'd not moved his ticket up, she went to the police.

Exhausted and worried, she spent her evenings at the bar, getting drunk and thinking of horrible scenarios: Kent murdered in an alley, Kent drowned in the river, Kent hit by a train or car because of that stupid mask. Each night she would stumble back to the loft and fall asleep.

One night, after passing out in bed, she awoke abruptly to find Kent sitting in a corner chair, staring at her, his masked face caught in a frame of silvery moonlight, disembodied.

Kent, she said, her eyes still a little blurry, her heart hitched between fear and relief, you're back.

The figure sat in the chair, the small murmur of breath patting against the mask.

Where were you? She asked. When again he didn't reply, she mumbled, Take it off.

He did not. She wondered if he was sleeping.

Kent, She said, a little louder. Seriously, it's fucking weird.

His head moved but he remained silent.

Take it off, she said again and when he didn't reply, she added, are you just staring at me?

An ugly expanse opened in her, a vast kind of empty she'd never known. Margot got up and began tossing her things into her backpack. She kept an eye on Kent, who turned his head as she moved about the room. When the bag was full, she slipped on her shoes and said, Say something or I'm leaving. The blood in Margot's face was throbbing and hot. Her pulse a hammer in her veins.

When it was clear he wasn't going to respond, Margot left.

Crossing through the courtyard, her body lightened in a way she'd not felt in months. As she reached the gate, she turned around for one last glimpse, perhaps in hopes something had changed, that Kent had taken off the mask, run down the stairs, followed her. Instead, she found him standing there, in the window, his masked head floating in all that awful black.

As Wide as Deep: a heart and a hole

With the yellow crescent moon slung in a strange way, they began digging a hole for the missing cat. Wider, she said, the cat is bigger. Though it absurd to dig a hole so large, he agreed. A gentleman's word is bond and a bond is a homely man's only hand to play. I'm sorry I was gone when she left, he said. She was my girl, she said. And you are mine, he said. Dig deep as my heart is wide, she said. He agreed. The further they went, the harder it was to displace the earth, until she took to the surface to pull and toss dirt. The moon was lost to him and he could only hear the chink and shush of the spade and huff of his breath. How long he'd been digging, how deep he had gone when he felt the first dump of damp soil hit his head. And another as he looked up. We're not burying the cat, are we? He asked. The spade slung in a strange way, he saw the moon righted, before she began to shovel again.

Supernova

The news moved through Juana's body filling her womb, pressing against her baby's head, against the uterine walls, pressing and circulating and winding tighter while expanding at the same time, dually whispering the doctor's information in English to Juana and to the fetus who did not yet know language and if born would not survive to learn. Sitting there, waiting for the words to make sense, to rearrange themselves and say anything that might have a different result, Juana remained silent. The doctor repeated herself in Spanish, but Juana did not understand Spanish.

When the doctor finished, Juana said, I heard you the first time.

It was clear this made the doctor uncomfortable, for she began scribbling notes in a Juana's file. Part of Juana wanted to know what the doctor was writing; but what did it matter in the end? Juana had a fetus in her womb who was viable enough to survive gestation, but not so viable to survive life outside her body.

What are my options?

I'm afraid you'll have to carry the pregnancy to term.

A child in a distant room screamed and someone spoke in the next room, his sonorous voice vibrating in the wall as if it were trying to escape and come to her. When does a fetus become a child, she wondered. For a moment she held the words *fetus* and *baby* in her head, but they chipped and crumbled before coming out. Language had never felt so conditional, so fragile. Raising a hand to her belly, rubbing it, she said, There, there.

Juana had done everything to ensure the fetus' safety, eating healthier, reading children's books aloud, doing yoga, cooing to the fetus. Juana asked if she should quit doing these things and the doctor suggested she continue because God worked in mysterious ways and the baby could, after all, survive.

Then there's a small chance he could make it?

I didn't mean to give you the wrong idea, Juana. It's not likely, but God has His ways.

It seemed God did have His ways and one of those ways was to kill her child in a desperate, terrifying few seconds after its birth. Anger streaked through her because she'd always obeyed God. Followed His rules. While her friends drank and slept around in their teens, Juana had taken care of her grandmother, walked with her to church in the summer mornings, prayed alongside her, sang with her. Yet her friends had healthy babies in their teens and early twenties. Here was Juana, married, chaste until wedding night, young enough, swollen with a fetus who would never be a baby. Her hand rubbed her belly again. There, there.

As Juna sat on the bench outside the clinic, she considered the best way to tell Cullen. This would devastate him. When the pregnancy test came back positive, he'd been more excited than she. When they'd learned the sex, he'd bought cigars for all his friends. Maybe Cullen could drive her to a clinic in another town for a second opinion if he could borrow a car from someone at work—his supervisor maybe. No, even his car was a rust bucket, the tires bald.

Juana waited at the kitchen table for Cullen to return from work. When the night came, she did not stand to turn on the light for only the living needed light and despite her beating heart, her pumping lungs, and her burning eyes, she did not feel like one of the living. By the time Cullen arrived, exhaustion had wrung him through. Placing his lunch box on the table, he took a seat.

Did I forget something?

You did not.

Why are you waiting for me in the dark?

With her left hand, she rubbed her belly, felt the fetus move inside her. Cullen did not deserve this news. He was the kindest person she'd ever met. It wasn't she who wept at the end of romance movies, but he. It wasn't she who fed the birds, the squirrels, the stray dogs, who volunteered for church events, who nursed a wounded bird to health, who donated blood, but Cullen. There was little she could say in the matter of the fetus that wouldn't break his heart, wouldn't take an already weathered young man and age him further. Every week, he took on more hours, saving as much as he could to ensure their baby would have food and clothing, have a crib and a mobile above its bed. Juana thought of the fetus in her, floating in all that fluid, curled comfortably, waiting for its journey into the world. Again, she thought of its agony.

In an article she'd read about pregnancy complications, the author wrote forty percent of marriages ended after a child dies during childbirth. Juana wasn't sure why the author had needed to insert that statistic and sitting there in the kitchen with Cullen staring at her, she wished she could slap them. She couldn't bear the thought of life without Cullen. They'd been together since before she'd had her first period. He was all she knew. And still she needed to tell him. Every time she attempted to broach a conversation that might lead her toward a gentle transition, she could only think to say, *Please don't leave me*. The refrigerator compressor kicked on and they both turned to look.

Thing's loud.

The fetus is going to die.

For a few seconds, Cullen didn't speak. He just started through the twilight at the fridge. I should start looking for a new compressor, he said.

Hadn't he heard her? She'd said it loud enough.

Did you hear me, I said our fetus is going to die.

I heard you.

The frustration in Cullen's voice nearly pulled her asunder. Tears began to well in her eyes, but she inhaled and cleared them with the back of her hand.

What am I supposed to do with that? Hi, honey, welcome home. Our baby's going to die.

Fetus.

This what the doctor said?

There was a chasm forming between them already and Juana felt its pull towards the bottom, could practically see Cullen on the rim turning and walking away.

Once the fetus leaves my body, he will die.

Lowering his head, Cullen pulled his ballcap off and ran his fingers through his hair. We can see another doctor, get a second opinion. Surely something can be done.

Then the reality hit him. They were two hours from the next free clinic. Neither of them could rent a car and they didn't know anyone who owned one that would make such a long trip. Cullen knew this too. Maybe saying these things made him feel less helpless. Without another word, he grabbed a beer from the fridge, leaned against the kitchen sink, and closed his eyes. The crack of the top shot through the room, piercing Juana.

I don't want to lose you, she said between breaths.

Swift and sure, Cullen was at her side, holding her face in his hands and kissing her cheek. You'll never lose me, he said.

The voice came two nights after telling Cullen the news. It was quiet at first, a whisper, and when it had come to her, she was certain it was the neighbor's TV. Setting her knitting down, she cocked her head to see if she could hear the voice again. At first, nothing, but as she raised her needles, it came again. *Help*, it said. The voice was child-like but not a child's—a voice spun round a post and pulled until it grew so high pitched, it was nearly inaudible. But it *was* audible and she'd heard it. Setting the knitting on the cushion next to her, she walked around the living room, placing her ear against the walls. In one she heard the neighbor's shower; in the next, she heard only her pulse; in the following, the whirl of a hair dryer, and the last, the patter of rain. Still, the voice came again once she moved back to the center of the room. It was close. Too close. As if coming not from inside the apartment but coming from inside her.

She felt foolish, but she asked, What did you say?

Help, it said.

You're hurting?

No.

Have you hurt?

No.

Will you hurt?

Yes.

The fetus in her belly kicked. It had never kicked before.

Did you kick?

Another kick came.

She rubbed her belly, sat down and continued to ask questions but found the fetus had stopped speaking to her. She wondered if it were possible for a fetus to communicate. Had it gathered some language from all the books she'd read to it? No, the fetus was not speaking to her. She was being irrational. However, as she convinced herself of this, she could not help but feel distant from the fetus growing inside of her. Hadn't there been more miraculous things in the Bible? Why did it seem so impossible a fetus growing inside of her, sharing her food, her blood, her breath could share her words? The fetus kicked and Juana took this as a sign.

The next day, Cullen took Juana out for dinner at the only restaurant that wasn't fast food or a bar, and though its tablecloths were faded and its décor two decades out of fashion, she was happy to be out of the house and sitting among local couples who spoke in hushed voices. The past few days they'd spent turns crying, Cullen more than she. As the reality of the pending death dawned on him, she found herself growing frustrated with the wait. It seemed ludicrous to wait for the fetus to pass from her.

Let's go to New Mexico, Juana said.

We ain't got a way there.

I bet we can find someone to give us a lift to Alpine. Take the bus from there.

Why New Mexico?

Juana drug a biscuit through gravy, moving it in subtle undulations. I was just thinking why wait?

Wait to go on a vacation?

Dropping the biscuit, she said, Wait for the baby to die.

Cullen looked around the restaurant, his shoulders slightly hunched as if Juana had shouted it, as if the patrons had all turned and stared. But she didn't and they hadn't and why would it matter anyway?

Don't say that, Cullen said.

Why not?

It's one thing our baby is going to die; it's another to kill it.

It don't make a bit of difference, Cullen.

We can go to jail for one. There's a difference. Leaning back in his chair, Cullen drank his draft beer. The glass had always reminded Juana of a young woman's body, buxom at the top and bottom with a slender waist. She wondered if she'd get her figure back once the fetus was gone.

We can't kill our baby, Cullen said.

It's only a baby if I give birth to it.

Dropping his stained napkin on the table, Cullen said, Let's not talk about this now.

She wasn't hungry, but picked her biscuit back up and began eating it. When would they talk about it if not then, she wondered. She'd tried bringing it up before, but then Cullen began staying at work later than ever, and when he came home, he drank and cried. She'd been so worried about pushing him, she'd kept the discussions light, and here he was again, sober and present but unwilling to talk about the fetus.

As Juana chewed her soggy bread, the voice came again, *Help*.

Yes, she said aloud, rubbing her stomach.

She and Cullen ate the rest of their meal in silence, a world of distance between them. If she told Cullen she'd been hearing the fetus in her head, he'd surely think she'd lost her mind. Still, she wanted to tell him. They always told each other everything despite how difficult it was, and everything sometimes required extreme vulnerability. Cullen had told her what his uncle had done to him when he was a child, how he'd sometimes awake thinking his uncle was atop him, sweating, how he never really believed the man was dead even though he'd seen the body lowered into the ground. That couldn't have been easy. And she'd told him she'd stolen money from the till after old man Pérez had a heart attack. Even as she recalled it, she was overcome by a wave of guilt, and despite having atoned for the sin in confession, she believed the old man would still be alive if she'd called the doctor before she'd taken the money. Maybe, Juana thought, this is her punishment. Then, she began spiraling, each thought darker and more damning than the one before.

I love you, Cullen said. Juana nearly missed it and when she didn't respond immediately, he said, I'm not mad.

Reaching her hand out, she took his between her fingers and smiled so he knew she wasn't mad either, and like that, she felt seen and the thoughts abated.

As the weeks passed, the fetus began to speak and use more words. Lying in bed one Sunday morning, she waited to see if the fetus would speak, and when Cullen awoke asking her why she was rubbing her belly and starting at the ceiling, she replied she wasn't yet ready to start her routine. The morning light and the sputtering call of a canyon wren filled her heart with a thrilling quiver. Cullen's face was bathed in gold light and she didn't dare speak for ruining the moment. She lifted her hand and touched his nose with her index finger, which he pulled to his lips and kissed.

I dreamed you had our boy, Cullen said. Then, as his words dawned on him, he said, Christ, I'm sorry.

Juana wasn't sure why, but his dream didn't upset her. In that space, that time, that sun, and the presence of the singing wren, she found herself occupying a state of contentment she'd never known.

I was thinking, she said, if I told you I would suffer an agonizing death upon stepping outside this house, what would you do?

I'd want to know the particulars, he said. It was clear in his voice he knew she was talking about the fetus he called their boy. He'd called it their boy since the day they'd found out the sex, and when he found out the boy would die, he continued to call it their boy or sometimes their son. He'd even talked about making a casket for him by hand so they could have people over for a wake and funeral as if watching the child die wasn't bad enough. Juana knew he'd only been trying to help, and when she'd kindly asked him what the fuck he'd been thinking, he was quick to see the folly of his suggestion.

The particulars don't matter. It's just the facts. I go outside, I suffer.

I'd keep you inside, bring the world to you until we figured it out. The dying thing.

He was being a good sport. Cullen was almost always a good sport. Pulling his hand into hers, and locking their fingers she said, And if I couldn't stay; if I was forced out?

Who's forcing you, Cullen said and when she didn't reply, he nodded and said, the particulars don't matter. Quirking his mouth in thought, he pumped Juana's hand twice in a manner she could only interpret as a plead for her to let him out of this, but she couldn't because he needed to know the impossibility of her heart, growing and cracking at once all the time.

I'd be devastated.

But you could give me a quick death, a dignified and silent death.

That's murder.

Not if I want it.

Then suicide.

Not if you do it.

You can't fool God, he said.

God would understand. The state of Texas—

Standing and walking to the dresser for his trousers Cullen said, I can't do this anymore. It's killing me too, you know?

Juana wanted to tell him she understood, to tell him it was killing her more because only she heard the fetus begging her day after day to act before it was too late. Please, she finally said, please consider. There's a bus from Alpine. You don't have to go.

We're going to miss mass if we don't leave. He softened his voice and said, I'll make sure nothing happens to you. This was his dove, his fig leaf. Despite her desire to press a little further, she did not. When he left the room, the fetus spoke, *Suffer little children.*

Yes, Juana said, but he believes in miracles.

Juana and Cullen arrived late to mass and took the last two pews where the town drunks and whores often sat to get out of the heat for a spell. The priest was a kindly old man who believed anyone who desired God's shelter could come out of the heat and listen to his words. Parishioners never looked kindly on those in last pews and despite the fact they knew Juana and Cullen well, they gave them the same deference when they'd been instructed to turn to their neighbors and shake their hands.

Peace be with you, Cullen said to Mrs. Fontane.

And also with you, she sneered.

When it came time for the transubstantiation, the fetus began speaking. *His breath,* the fetus said. She wondered if the fetus could hear her thoughts. *Whose breath,* she thought, but the fetus did not reply. As Cullen stood for communion, Juana seized the opportunity to say, Whose breath?

Bad breath, the fetus said.

What did the fetus mean, Juana wondered. Did she have bad breath? Maybe it was Cullen.

What breath, Cullen said.

Without responding to his question, Juna went to take communion. Perhaps, she thought, God's body, God's blood, will bring a kindly curse to her body for a miscarriage. He works in mysterious ways, everyone told her. Certainly he did. Why else would she be forced to carry a dying thing to term? What good came from that?

As she knelt before the priest and he placed God's body upon her tongue. He said, The body of Christ.

The drab golden scrim on either side of their second-hand crucifix fluttered in the air as the rotating fan hit it. Christ there upon the cross looked so worn, so heartbroken by his father's betrayal. What father would see his child suffer so, Juana said.

Father Miguel looked to form a response but did not answer her question. Bless you, he said and handed his bowl to the Deacon.

She remained kneeling there for the fetus told her to remain. Father Miguel returned to the ambo, another hand me down from one of the bigger churches east of them. She'd once found its chipped stain and cracked sides charming but now found it sad. The whole world seemed to reveal its darkness to her lately. Had the world always been filled with shadows, she thought, or dirt? How quickly her perspective changed. Father Miguel cleared his throat and Juana found the congregation watching her, waiting for her to return to her seat. Stumbling over her feet, she stood and walked back. Every eye from every pew moved with her.

After the ceremony, the parishioners gathered under the trees for a potluck. Father Miguel found Juana and asked her if she might like to talk. They walked to his shabby dark office in the back of the church where she sat on a folding chair next to a chipped and faded mint green wall.

You asked me a question during communion, he said.

I did.

Are you questioning your faith?

No, Father.

Are you questioning God.

Yes, Father.

I knew your grandmother well, so I know you understand why God sacrificed his only child.

Bad Breath, the fetus said.

God has cursed me.

God has blessed you, Juana. You swell with proof of his love, for where there is God there is life.

Bad father.

Which father, Juana wondered. The holy father, the priest, or Cullen? She wanted to ask but knew well enough this time not to speak the question aloud.

My fetus will die painfully upon its birth, she said.

Father Miquel placed his hand atop Juana's and said, Every mother has a fear their child—

The doctor told us.

The Father's eyes seemed to move back in his skull, his mouth fell limp. Then he smiled and said, We need to pray.

Ow. Ow. Ow, yelled the fetus, startling Juana.

Does it hurt, she said.

You're being childish, Father Miguel said.

Help, said the fetus.

Juana stood from her chair and said, I'm sorry, Father. I'm not well today.

When she found Cullen, he'd already eaten three cobs of corn, and skins clung to his teeth when he smiled. She walked past him and he followed until they were home.

After Cullen left for work the next morning, Juana left him a note and walked to the gas station where she proceeded to ask everyone who came through if they were headed to Alpine. Around noon, Mrs. White arrived and said she was happy to have company on her trip to Alpine. Juana bought them both cold sodas and a bag of pork rinds and they left. For two hours they didn't speak. Mrs. White's car had a fine radio and they listened to old songs and sometimes sang with them. The fetus tapped inside her.

It was on the bus ride some hours later when the fetus began speaking to Juana again. It asked questions, expressed its dislike of pork rinds and its love of soda. How quickly the fetus was learning, perceiving the world through gentle sounds and foreign flavors. Sometimes Juana would sing answers to the fetus while the bus rolled through the dry Texas landscape. No one judged a woman for singing, but should she speak to herself they'd turn their heads. The fetus enjoyed it when Juana took baths, when she walked in the evenings, when she laughed. It did not, however, like it when she and Cullen were intimate. This made Juana blush and sing Brenda Lee's "I'm sorry." The old woman behind her enjoyed this song and asked her to continue singing. Though Juana didn't remember all the words, she invented new ones and the woman didn't seem to notice.

Night had fallen by the time they reached El Paso, and the city sparkled in the distance before a mouth full of buildings consumed them. She'd never been to a city so large and found herself in disbelief that so many could live in one place. At the station, a police officer in a cowboy hat watched people getting off the buses. When Juana stepped off, he pulled her away.

Papers, he said.

Papers, she said.

Tus papeles de inmigración.

Juana did not speak Spanish. Her grandmother forbade her from learning. If she spoke only English, her grandmother reasoned, she'd have an easier time fitting in.

I'm American, she said then pulled her ID out of her purse.

He looked at it carefully. Though it was dark, he wore a pair of shooting glasses. His arms were strong and the biceps budged where he'd pegged the sleeves of his shirt. His gut hovered over his belt, firm and hard as a stone. As he handed the ID back to her, he said, Ticket? She showed it to him. Raising an untamed eyebrow over his lens, he said, I'm afraid you'll need to come with me.

I'm a citizen.

Ain't that, come now.

Run, said the fetus.

Juana followed the man but the further they got from the bus, the louder the fetus began to urge her to run. She wanted to ask him if he heard it, surely it was loud enough now that it penetrated the world outside. However, he did not seem to hear the fetus, and as he opened the back door to his cruiser, she tried to run but the man was too quick.

Once he'd secured her in the back, he sat in the driver's seat where he looked back through the cage. Under the depot lights his brow and nose cut harsh shadows on his face. Working a piece of gum in his mouth, he ticked at her.

The fetus spoke to her in a whisper, *He wants to cause us harm.*

Though Juana was scared to speak, she said, Why are you holding me?

He wants to cause us harm.

I'm just giving you time to think.

He will take us to a second location.

I want a lawyer.

The man's lip rose over his teeth. I have to take you in for that.

He will take us to a second location and harm us.

Time to think for what?

Women in your condition, he said, come this way for a reason.

I'm going to see family.

No you ain't.

The bus began reversing and Juana searched for a door handle. When she found none, she said, I'm going to miss my bus. The man waved goodbye to the bus. They sat there for some time before the man got out of the cruiser, walked over to her door, and opened it.

Juana climbed out but nearly fell over. The man grabbed her arm and she bucked against him.

I'm stranded, she said.

The man shut the door, walked around to the front and got in. As he reversed the car, he stopped, rolled down the window, and said, God bless, Ma'am.

By the time Juana made it back to town, it was midday. Her feet were blistered, her legs tired, and she'd sweat through her clothing. She'd never walked so many miles, but she'd had the fetus to sing to and the fetus often spoke to her along the way. Cullen got up from the kitchen table when she opened the door.

Are you okay? He said.

Tired.

And the boy?

And now you care about the fetus.

Goddamnit, I've always cared, Cullen said, taking her limp hand in his.

Juana knew this was true. He did care, but he was just too good natured to make the tough decisions, especially in the moments when legal and ethical stood at odds. He'd always been like this. Even when they were kids, he'd turn his back to injustices though they tore him up. If there were any flaw to him, Juana thought, it was this.

You need a nice warm bath, he said, leading her into the bathroom.

She could not argue with this, so she undressed as he ran a bubble bath and lit a candle. Though the water stung her blisters at first, the pain subsided by the time she sank into the water. She'd felt so dirty from the sweat and dust. Her body ached and her thoughts sat heavily in head. At least, she thought, the fetus will enjoy the bath.

Sitting on the toilet, Cullen asked her where she'd been and listened quietly as she explained. One of her favorite qualities about him was his ability to listen without interrupting or making faces. In the rare occasions he did, they were usually in public places, and Juana understood it wasn't a good habit to discuss personal matters in public anyway. After she finished, Cullen sat in silence. It was a calm silence, unlike her grandmother's silences which preceded unyielding criticism. Juana wouldn't blame Cullen if he was upset with her; she had attempted to make a choice without him. They'd always run big decisions by one another. She'd always trusted him before, so why the change now, she wondered. Was the fetus influencing her or did she know Cullen would never make the right decision? Part of her wanted to say he'd forced her hand, to ask him why he couldn't see what was coming, feel the way a father should, act to prevent undue suffering. She knew she should say something, but everything that came to mind seemed pointed and cruel. As she was about to say something, to break the silence with an apology she wasn't sure she'd mean, Cullen crawled down onto the floor next to the tub, held her face in his hands, and said, I'll try to get a car.

Juana could not sleep that afternoon despite feeling sick with exhaustion. As the fetus rambled on, she lay there in bed next to Cullen whose chest rose and sank with sleep. *He's lying*, the fetus said. Rubbing her belly, she hoped to soothe the fetus, but it only seemed to excite him. Each time she found herself drifting into sleep, the fetus would shout, jerking her awake. Please, she thought, just a few hours of sleep. The fetus would not listen.

The sun rose and Cullen left for work, but she found the more she tried to sleep, the louder the fetus grew. What can I do, she said, but the fetus would not answer directly. Instead, he asked her if she wanted him to suffer. Of course she did not, but this did not seem to please the fetus. She tried to calm the fetus, taking hot baths, singing, eating sweets but nothing worked. When Cullen came home, the fetus began shouting whenever he'd speak. Using contextual clues, Juana attempted to respond to Cullen, but often the words of the fetus would infect her sentences. It was clear to her Cullen was losing patience for her odd answers, so she found herself apologizing, blaming it on exhaustion, on the pregnancy, on sun stroke, but never on the fetus screaming inside of her. Cullen, kind as ever, kissed her head and said he'd make dinner to let her rest on the couch.

While he toiled in the kitchen and she lay prostrate upon the sofa, a muted ache formed in her back, followed by one in her pelvis. It faded after a few seconds. It is just dehydration, Juana thought.

She was still recovering from the long hot walk. Then it came again, stronger this time. As she inched up with her elbows, she saw her dress spot, and then at once, go dark with water.

Cullen, she said. Labor.

Rushing into the room with a wooden spoon dripping with cream sauce, he found her there wet and squirming to get up. It had grown so difficult to move with the fetus swelling inside her. Cullen went to her side and helped her off the couch. Standing there pale and moon-eyed, he ran through some lines he'd learned from the childbirth classes at the local rec center, but couldn't seem to remember the order: drive carefully, bring clothes, don't panic, call the doctor, be supportive. All that preparation and he was reduced to a child in the moment. Ambulance, he said finally.

The fetus screamed, its words no longer human, but something primordial and angry. She should have tried harder, should have walked across the border and thumbed her way up to Las Cruces. Louder and louder it screamed until its voice ripped through her and she fainted.

When she came to, she was in the county hospital, Cullen and the doctor discussing a cesarean birth.

I don't need one, she said. Though part of her wanted to be unconscious, she knew it was only right she be there in the child's time of need.

Are you sure, the doctor said.

Yes.

Her body contracted again, the pain far more intense than before, taking her breath away. A nurse saw her struggling and cooed for her to breathe in a rhythmic pattern. What the nurse could not see was the fetus digging its fingers into her. He doesn't want to leave, Juana said.

The nurse dotted her forehead with a cloth and said, It's time.

They began coaching her and she followed their directions. Maybe, she thought, the fetus will beat the odds. Once birthed, maybe it will open its tiny eyes, expand its lungs, and cry, not from pain but from the shock of leaving the womb. She pushed and she pushed. Cullen held her hand and said things like "good job," "you're doing it," and "one more," and eventually it was one more as the fetus left her body and became a boy. For a moment the child was silent, blinking against the cruel light. Yes, she thought, steady on, child. However, as Cullen began to speak, a smile wide upon his face, the child began convulsing, a pained look of confusion on its face, twisting into a broken mask, as the child raged against the pain filling its body. Then the screaming, the god-awful bloody screams of an infant's tiny lungs. There were no tears, no cries, just piercing screams while his small arms raged against his chest as if trying to pull it open. Please, Juana thought, make it stop, but no one did They held the poor thing in their hands, talking to it as if it could understand the flawed constructs of human reason, and let it suffer for far too long.

Juana pushed against the bed, pushed against Cullen's hands as they restrained her. If they wouldn't put the child out of its misery, she would; however, as she cleared Cullen's grasp, the child released one last scream which seemed to tear its lungs apart and fell silent.

Juana's husband wept but she did not. There was, it seemed, nothing left inside her. The nurse attempted to wrap the small corpse, to move it from view, but Juana stopped them, told them to unwrap the body (not so that she could find closure but so that her husband might). Or was there something else at play within her, some feeling of resentment stowed deep inside her and released when the fetus passed into the world of air and light.

The fetus, now a dead child, lay there among the soiled towels, its body glistening, still and pruney. Cullen continued to weep and only asked them to carry the child away once it seemed he'd run out of tears.

Diastasis recti her doctor had told her weeks after she'd passed the fetus. With exercise and diet the muscles might return to their normal shape, but surgery might be required a few months down the road. Juana waited patiently after, counting her calories, walking, doing exercises, monitoring herself in the mirror. When three months had passed, it seemed her belly was still growing and Juana was sleeping less and less.

I think it's sexy, her husband said when she'd first complained about it.

She knew this was true; he'd said as much when she'd first developed a baby bump months before. Still, she hated it—hated the belly because the belly came without a voice this time and she missed the voice. By the fifth month she was waddling, her feet and back aching. One night, as she lay upon her side on the couch massaging her feet against the arm, her husband came home and sat upon the coffee table and stared at her for a few moments—his lips pulled tight, his brown drawn together.

We need to talk to the doctor about that surgery, he said.

Surgery now, she said, her tone an accusation, a battering ram, a finger on the calendar to the day she'd asked for an abortion.

It's not natural.

She wasn't sure how healthy any of it was—having a child on their income, letting the fetus pass into the world only to scream and die, going on with life after as if they'd not witnessed the cruelly of the world. What would the fetus say now, she wondered. Since the voice had left her, the world had been turned inside out, all meaning removed, all drive and emotion gone save for her growing resentment. It was unfair and she knew it. Her husband had never said a cruel word to her, had loved that fetus he called a child, had finally offered to help it even though it was too late. Juana knew he was right, it was unnatural, likely unhealthy, and it did nothing but remind him of what he'd lost.

I will not, she said.

They can give you something for sleep.

I will not go.

Her husband did not understand. He reapproached, said it in a new way, softened his voice, knelt beside her. When this did not garner the answer he desired, he said he'd carry her there. Again, this did not work, so he said he'd carry her there for her own good. With effort, Juana swung her feet onto the floor and waddled into the bathroom, closing the door behind her. He followed, knocked on the door for a while, apologized, then went into the bedroom and eventually fell asleep—his snores creeping through the wall.

The following morning Juana remained in the bathroom until her husband left. Most of the day she wandered around their dingy little apartment unable to see the charm she'd seen in it before. She scrubbed at the counters for a while, but the stains from previous tenants did not lighten. She vacuumed the shag carpets but they did not raise, did not look less soiled. Even when she lit a candle, the musty smell did not abate. Everything lacked the sparkle of life, the joy of living. It was all dirt and shadows.

Who was to blame for this? Cullen? The doctor who let it get this far, who despite knowing better refused to provide the child mercy? The men who made laws? The police officer who stopped her in El Paso? Or was she to blame—her diet, her genetics, her choice of God? She could not choose who to blame as it seemed she could blame everyone and no one. If only the fetus still spoke to her, it could tell her who to blame. It could tell her what to do. And what would the fetus say to her?

Closing her eyes, Juana tried to calm her thoughts. If only she could quiet the world, she might still hear the fetus. Surely, some small part of it must remain inside her. Her breath pumped inside her, the fridge hummed, the water hissed in the walls, but nothing inside her womb spoke. Listen harder, she said. When she again heard nothing but domestic sounds, she paced the house and an unfamiliar feeling rose in her—a desire to collapse, to pull at her hair, or smash a window, all of it coursing through her, swirling in her stomach until she grew sick and dizzy and collapsed on the couch where she pulled a pillow over her face.

She'd been up all night in the bathroom, sitting in the hard bathtub, her neck bent, her knees pressed against the porcelain. Her thoughts clouded her mind and grew heavier in the dark behind her eye lids. Her body began growing lighter and just before she found sleep, a voice came to her and spoke a single word, *everyone.* Juana's eyes snapped open.

Had she really heard it? *Say it again,* she thought and when the fetus did not reply, she spoke it. Again, the voice did not come to her. Perhaps she'd only imagined she'd heard it, a part of a dream forcing its way into her world—something meant for her. Perhaps then, it was only through dreams the fetus could speak across the threshold of the dead. However, Juana did not sleep. She was close but still awake.

It was true though, whether the fetus had said it or not, there was enough blame to go around and despite her love for Cullen, despite his kindness, he should have been there, should have helped their fetus so that it would not have felt pain. Her belly hurt, a searing white pain, as if the fetus were cutting its way out with a dull knife. Yes, Juana said, there, there. The pain stopped abruptly, and she patted her stomach.

Arriving home from work late, Cullen was thinworn and covered with dirt. He kissed Juana on the head and sat down in the recliner where he promptly began snoring. Still after all these months, he was working the same hours he'd worked while saving for the child who'd only breathe for a few moments. Surely, he could stop if he wanted, but maybe he didn't want to, maybe he was avoiding home. His chest rose and sank as he slept. Again, he slept peacefully while she stumbled through the apartment half lucid. Working to her feet and coggling over to him, Juana slid his nose between her fingers and pinched lightly. Cullen's chest rose and rose until he turned his head and snorted, breaking her hold.

Juana returned to the bathroom and lay in the tub. The cool touch of the porcelain calmed her. Perhaps the voice would return to her. Juana tried to remember what the voice had sounded like. Sometimes she remembered it being high pitched and other times she remembered it being scratchy. She didn't like the scratchy voice. A fetus wouldn't speak that way—in a voice like an old woman strapped to a chair. It seemed unfair that she was already forgetting the voice of something living in her, something made of her.

The neighbor's dog howled and Juana counted the owner's steps from one room to the next. When he arrived, he yelled at the dog, and though she could not make out the words, she felt them in the thin walls. Poor dog, she thought, cooped up in that apartment. She was trapped too. Trapped in their drab little apartment, always awake. Everything had grown foreign in her sleeplessness—sound, touch, taste, thought—all of it feeding back inside her head like a mirror maze in a funhouse. It had become suffocating. Rubbing her hands along the bathroom tiles, she lost herself in the sensation and wondered if this was what it felt like to be high. She'd never tried drugs, never drunk to excess, and when she'd given birth, if she could call it that, she refused sedatives or shots.

The next evening Cullen returned home with the doctor. They each pulled chairs up to the couch where Juana sat knitting a small beanie. The doctor's face softened, her eyes sloping down towards her checks.

Juana, she said, why haven't you visited me?

I need more time with it, Juana said. With what Juana wasn't quite sure. With the grief? With what was growing inside of her? With the feeling of being a mother? All of it and none of it all at once. More than anything Juana wanted to be left alone—alone so she could listen, so she might hear that small, fragile voice once more.

There is something wrong, Cullen said.

Let's get you to the hospital for some scans, the doctor said.

Is it an emergency, Juana said.

Not per se.

I'm not ready, but I will go tomorrow.

The doctor is here with a car, Cullen said.

Please, Juana said.

The doctor held Cullen's gaze for a moment and they came to some agreement in that exchange. I can come by tomorrow, the doctor said. It's only a few miles.

Once the doctor left, Cullen and Juana went to bed, he sleeping easily and she wide awake in the desperate moonlight lying across her in a ghostly sash. She was tired, her stomach nothing but acid, her hands shaky. Why, she wondered, can't I sleep? Why was it she was left to suffer with this alone? Cullen had cried and moved on and now he wanted to remove all evidence the pregnancy had happened. She was alone and the only one who understood was the fetus. What would it say?

She thought about the scans, she thought about the surgery, the doctors meddling in her womb after they'd been so reluctant to enter before. She would not let them, would reason with Cullen in the morning, tell him she needed to see this through. What exactly this was, she wasn't sure, but knew it was meant to happen, a gift of some kind, perhaps left by the fetus for the fetus knew she'd tried, that she'd cared. The rest of the night, she sat in the kitchen and steeled herself against what would come. She would resist, Cullen would insist, and the doctor would join in with all her logic. All that logic and still the doctor couldn't help Juana in her time of need. How hard would it have been, Juana wondered, for the doctor to do what was right? No one would have known, just Juana, Cullen, and the doctor. Maybe a nurse, if they really needed it.

The morning came and Cullen entered the kitchen with a small bag packed for Juana. As he started a pot of coffee, he said, Doc should be here soon.

Juana didn't speak at first. She'd grown so tired, she had nearly convinced herself she was dreaming.

Damn nice of her to offer the ride.

I'm not going, Juana said in a voice so small, she wasn't sure if she'd said anything at all.

Pulling two mugs from the cupboard, Cullen began humming. A knock came at the door and Cullen let the doctor in. I'm making coffee, he said. Figured you might want a cup.

I'd love a cup, the doctor said.

I said I'm not going, Juana said, standing and approaching the counter.

She is, Cullen said to the doctor.

Don't speak for me, Juana said. Everything seemed hollow—Cullen, the doctor, the counter, all of it hollow. Placing her hand on the counter, she knocked on it, rubbed her hand over the smooth Formica until she hit the cutlery block they'd bought at a yard sale.

I understand your reservations, the doctor began, her words soft as if speaking to a child, but we're just doing scans today.

Cullen's gone and packed a night bag, Juana said running her fingers along the knife handles, finding their beveled edges intoxicating. Pulling one out, she tried to remember its use—steak, bread, fruit. Why couldn't she remember? In her mind the words seemed to ripple and collapse inside themselves.

Just in case, Cullen said, grabbing Juana's wrist. He'd done this countless times, always gentle.

Again, the cutting pain came in her stomach and she nearly buckled, pulling the cutlery block over, spilling knives on the counter and floor. All the sounds reverberated inside of her, all of it cave-like and strange. Juana's knees trembled as the pain came again and she slipped from the counter. The doctor rushed to catch her, but slipped and fell onto the floor, saying something in a strange exhale as if out of breath, as the knives rattled below them—all of the noise bouncing around inside Juana, all of it sharp and awful. What was the doctor saying, Juana wondered.

They squirmed on the floor for a while, each of them trying to get their footing. Juana was first up, but the doctor could not for the doctor had a knife in her. How had she fallen on a knife, Juana wondered.

Cullen said something, his voice a barb, but Juana couldn't tell what he'd said. Language and knives and bodies were making the same noises, angles and edges and all hollow. He knelt next to the doctor, talking to her, saying something. Turning to Juana, he shouted, but she could not understand him. Towel, towel, towel, he repeated.

Juana wanted to sleep. She had lost the world, lost its texture, its sound, its beauty. Outside, Juana thought, morning air might help. Stepping outside, she—swollen with something other than a child, something without a pulse, a kick, a voice—began walking along the street until it led to another, then another, and before long she'd wended and turned enough she was on the outskirts of their small town, edging the state road, a specter among the cattle. With her hands on her belly, she cooed, There, there, as she had many times, waiting always for the fetus to speak to her, but was met only by the abject silence of a woman who'd failed to produce a viable child, failed to take mercy on that which did live briefly inside her. She walked on, day to day, night to night, beyond the next town, beyond the one after, westerly, ignoring good men who'd offered her a ride, the police who'd asked if she was okay, the other wanderers she passed along the way, until she came upon a forestland where she left the road and slipped between the trees, until she found a small flowing river and stepped into the babbling waters. The algae below the stream was green and soft.

I shall lie here, she thought, lie and sleep. Kneeling, she eased her body back into the water. Her skull sank into the gentle mud and water rushed around her head where beneath the surface, the world fell silent save for the curl and whisper of the current. She was so very tired and water was cool and pure and she would just lay for a little while. Her eyes closed, breath grew calm, and the world lost its gravity. Just a little while she said and was gone.

ИЗ ПЛОТИ И ШЕРСТИ

Translated by Alisa Kuzmina

I.

Хоть мне и было одиноко, я не нуждался в компании койотов. Я зашторил окна. Убедился, что банки с консервами были в гараже. Не оставил ничего, что могло бы приманить их ко мне. И все равно они пришли. Фырча и взвизгивая, они скребли окна и двери.

Городская застройка вынудила их сменить место обитания. Ходили слухи о неудачном научном эксперименте. Информация так и не подтвердилась, но в новостях говорили, будто в их стае видели ребенка. Ведущие посмеивались. Советовали звонить в службу опеки. Говорили, что у некоторых людей слишком много свободного времени, чего только им не привидится. На самом деле они понятия не имели, с чем имели дело. Таков был компромисс жизни в маленьком городе. Безопасность в обмен на отсутсвие критического мышления. В конце концов, науке были известны случаи воспитания детей дикими собаками. Волками. Бездомными кошками. Взять ту же легенду о Пекосе Билле. Но насколько это возможно? Прожить так целый год?

Вынести беспощадную зиму? Странное чувство посетило меня тогда, чей-то призрачный рот жевал мой палец.

Я закрыл двери. Запер решетки на окнах. Захлопнул гараж. Я лежал на диване, уставившись на кухонный пол в соседней комнате. Думал о том, как раньше я подкармливал животных. Птиц. Белок. Койотов. Затем. Затем я подумал о ребенке в стае. Он пробегал мимо дома. Искал меня.

II.

В то время наука могла все. Люди рисовали в воздухе 3D ручками. Лечили заболевания стволовыми клетками. Прокладывали подводные железные дороги. Мы были частью новой эры. Эры исправления ошибок прошлого. Мы совершенствовали наши тела. Улучшали наши жизни.

Наша физиология не зависела от возраста. Почти. Ведь время меняет нашу личность. Реклама манипулирует нашими чувствами. Мы нервничаем. Злимся и скрепим зубами. Умиляемся маленьким детям. И как-то так вышло, что своими я не обзавелся. Ни жены, ни сыночка, ни лапочки-дочки. С моей смертью семейная линия превратится в пепел. Что ни капли не волновало меня в молодости. Я был слишком увлечен путешествиями. Тратой денег. Покупкой дома и хлама.

Мое желание завести ребенка возникло, когда я делал генеральную уборку. Перекладывал старые вещи из изношенных картонных коробок в гладенькие пластиковые контейнеры. Все было четко промаркировано. Это был занятный и красивый процесс. Ясные прямые линии света пронизывали пространство. В этих залежах картона и пластика я нашел снимок. Я маленький сижу у отца на коленке. Неужели я не видел фотографию раньше? А если видел, почему совсем о ней забыл?

Мой разум был не в силах восстановить то, что когда-то, возможно, знал. До тех пор. До тех пор, пока не вернулся к разбору вещей. В этом процессе каждая реликвия обретала новое значение. Это был архив редких сокровищ, в котором каждый снимок являлся драгоценностью, обрывок бумаги— священным объектом. Сначала я поместил их в отдельные папки. Пластиковые обложки служили им защитой. Все было пронумеровано и подсчитано. Что станет со всем этим? С этим домом из дерева, стекла и металла. С фотографиями моего отца. С воспоминаниями, которые он для меня сохранил. Исчезнет каждое слово?

Я лежал в кровати, как что-то кольнуло меня. Что-то в груди. Птица клюет. *Выпусти меня.* Той ночью мне приснилась коричневая река, впадающая в огромный белый океан. Течение несло меня к берегу. Волна повалила дерево и, когда я подплыл к самому устью, на меня обрушился поток воды. В этом крушении я услышал лишь одно слово: *ребенок.*

На следующий день, согласовывая счет для одного из клиентов, я все еще не мог выкинуть слово из головы. *Ребенок* я напечатал вместо *ребрышки.* Вместо *чай* я напечатал *чадо.* Мне нужно было проветриться. Съездить куда-нибудь пообедать. По пути в кафе, я проехал мимо центра искусственного оплодотворения. Немного подумав, я развернул машину.

Какое-то время мы говорили с женщиной из центра. Я отчетливо дал понять, что хочу стать донором спермы. Чей-то новорожденный тогда продолжил бы мою семейную линию. Я хотел рассказать о семейных воспоминаниях, которые мне хотелось бы сохранить, но она возразила. «Как нет?»—спросил я. «Нет», —повторила она. Моя ДНК будет конфискована, стерилизована и перекодирована. Им было нужно только мое семя. Все генетические маркеры при этом были бы стерты. Это показалось мне смешным. Наука зашла так далеко, но процесс зачатия был расшифрован ей не до конца. Им все еще был нужен биологический материал.

Тогда она дала мне визитную карточку коллеги—специалистки в сфере репродуктивного клонирования. «Клон?»—спросил я. «Да»,—ответила она.

Идея мне не понравилась. Я даже подумал не брать визитку. Но все-таки взял. А после, уже дома, выбросил ее в мусорное ведро.

Птица клюнула снова. Я пожевал губу. Хрустнул щиколотками. Обеспокоенный, я думал о рассказах из жизни моего отца. О драках в колледже. Футбольных победах. О том, как он учил меня наносить удар. Как рассказывал о солнечном сплетении, объясняя устройство человеческой анатомии. Я нащупал рукой грудину. Опустил кончик пальца в местечко под костью. Надавил.

Встреча с ученой состоялась на следующий день. В начале нашего разговора ей не удалось развеять все мои сомнения, и я почти направился к выходу, но она предложила мне кофе и слойку. По правде сказать, мысль о слойке очень обрадовала меня. Я остался, и мы продолжили обсуждать различные детали, связанные с клонированием.

К примеру, ребенка я получу уже младенцем. Его вынашивание произойдет в искусственной матке. Она также упомянула, что некоторых клонов называют *равнодушными*, поскольку они не имеют контакта с матерью. Затем она рассказала мне о теломерах. О проценте клонов, жизнь которых краткосрочна. О проценте аномалий. О генных дефектах, которые могут проявить себя с развитием малыша. «Да-да», сказал я, доедая слойку, затем попросил еще одну.

Месяцы ожидания ребенка я провел в подготовке дома. Покрыл монтажной пеной все острые углы. Подбил расшатавшиеся гвозди в половицах. Установил замки на дверцы шкафов. Затем. Затем я вынес вещи своей бывшей жены из комнаты для шитья. Построил детскую кроватку. Разрисовал стены. Облака, зверушки, звезды. Я пытался вспомнить, что я любил, будучи маленьким мальчиком. Что родители делали для меня. Я думал о том, как они красили стены в моей комнате. Как отец собирал кроватку. Какие надежды они, должно быть, возлагали. Пока все это не полетело к чертям. До алкоголя, драк, развода и смерти. И там, сидя на полу, я осознал, что могу все исправить.

Когда моя бывшая приехала за своей пыльной швейной машинкой, я был во дворе, насыпал еду в кормушки для белок. Раскладывал кукурузные зерна на маленьком столике. Мне очень нравилось наблюдать, как белки сидели на стульчике и обедали словно джентльмены, которым накрыли на стол. Она посмотрела на меня. «Ты все еще подкармливаешь их?»—спросила она. «Да»,—сказал я. «И койотов? Их ты тоже снова кормишь?» «Да»,—сказал я.

—

Она покачала головой и попросила разрешения зайти в дом проверить, не осталось ли там других ее вещей. Столько лет прошло. С тех пор, как она ушла на работу и больше уже не возвращалась. Нашла новый дом. Нового мужчину—«альфача», как называли его мои друзья. Он был копом. Делал мебель своими руками. Она родила от него двух мальчиков и девочку. А потом у нее, наверное, отсохла матка.

Я погрузил швейную машинку в багажник ее машины. На полу валялось несколько крекеров в форме зверушек. Подушка для детского кресла была заляпана многочисленными пятнами. Между сиденьями торчала трубочка от сока. Моя бывшая жена вышла во двор. «Что это?»—спросила она. «Что это что?»—спросил я. «Комната»,—сказала она. «У меня будет ребенок»,—сказал я. «Скоро?»—спросила она. «Да»,—ответил я. Она назвала меня сволочью. Дала мне пощечину. Спросила, почему я не хотел ребенка от нее. Ведь это все, что ей было нужно. Она же любила меня. Умоляла меня.

Что я мог ответить? Что хотел ребенка, чтобы передать ему

свои пожитки? Чтобы был кто-то, кто мог сохранить истории, ведущие свой путь со времен зарождения языка? Вместо этого я уставился на нее и ответил, что она права. Только это не помогло. Ее щеки покраснели. Она задала несколько уточняющих вопросов. О женщине. Докторе. Дате.

Я ответил на все попорядку. Она рассмеялась. Ее зубной ряд, широкий рот. Деревья покачнулись. Облака преградили солнечный свет. «Зачем тебе понадобился такой же, как ты?—спрашивала она,—со всеми твоими тревогами и генетическими несовершенствами?» «Я проложу ему дорогу в жизнь,—ответил я.—В отличие от моих родителей, у меня есть инструкция. Я смогу предоставить все, что нужно». Она лишь смеялась. И смеялась. Ее голос в моих ушах. Яд и злоба.

Я ударил ее по лицу перед тем, как осознал, что делаю. Она взглянула на меня, ощупывая щеку. Ее рот—трещина на гладком лице. Она ткнула пальцем мне в грудь и сказала: «ОТЛИЧНО». Затем села в машину и уехала.

В ту ночь я смотрел на звезды. Одна упала. Должно быть, разбилась где-то на том берегу реки, откуда доносился зов койотов. Перед тем как спокойно улечься на моей барабанной перепонке, их тоскливый, приглушенный клич переплетался меж крон деревьев, проносился по речной долине.

Покров ночи сгустился. Я думал о словах моей бывшей. О ее новом муже. Об их фото онлайн. Порадоваться их счастью было бы слишком. Вместо этого я хотел, чтобы его жизнь оборвалась каким-нибудь неожиданным способом. Пожар. Или выстрел. Несущаяся на него комета. Я посмотрел на стол, который стоял во дворе—мой подарок ко дню ее рождения. Я помню, как купил древесину. Распаковал пилу. Нашел в интернете информацию о том, как наносить эпоксидную смолу. В свете луны мне были видны все его неровности. Кривое уродство по сравнению с идеальной двуспальной кроватью, которую этот альфач сделал из срубленного им дерева.

———

Я приподнял угол стола и толкнул его. Стол с треском упал. Вдалеке меж деревьев мелькнула пара глаз. Свет на веранде ловко поймал в них свое отражение. От чувства, что за мной следят, меня одолела тревога. Глаза койотов снова мигнули, я слышал их дыхание, шорох лап. Я пошел в гараж. Вытащил несколько ведерок собачьего корма. Поставил их у обочины. Прошмыгнул в дом. Они пришли. Сначала один. Двое. Еще один. Наконец все пятеро собрались вокруг мисок, сопя, рыча, взвизгивая. Глаза их лихорадочно горели.

III.

Когда настало время ехать за ребенком, меня одолело то самое смешение чувств, которое наверняка знакомо многим новоиспеченным родителям. Пока мальчик рос в инкубаторе, волнений у меня не было. Не было тревожных снов. Никаких мыслей о деформированных головах. Отказывающих легких. Слепоте. Я подготавливал дом без особых переживаний. Покупал подгузники, думая о ребенке, как о вещи, но не о человеке, жизнь которого могла закончиться по ряду причин. Причин, число которых начало множиться в моих мыслях, вытесняя всякий здравый смысл.

Мне потребовалось несколько попыток, чтобы наконец приехать за ним. Там, где я должен был повернуть налево, я поворачивал направо. Должен был остановиться, вместо этого ускорялся, чуть не сбил парня на велосипеде. А вдруг моего мальчика кто-нибудь собьет? Похитит. Надругается над ним. В тот момент мир стал невыносим. Я не помню, как приехал в клинику.

Каким-то образом я оказался перед стеклянной дверью. Подошел секретарь. Открыл ее. «Вы в порядке? Дверь не открывается?» Я смотрел на него, пытаясь вымолвить: «Все отлично, открывается», но смог сказать только *аборт*.

Ко мне поднесли мальчика. Он был завернут в бежевое. Гендерно нейтральный цвет. Можно подумать они не знали, какого пола он будет. В сантиметрах от меня малыш спал на руках у ученой. «Ваш ребенок»,—сказала женщина. Хотя мое сознание дало команду *двигаться*, руки были прикованы к туловищу. «Сэр»,—продолжала она. Мальчик повернул головку. Его розовые веки—кусочки плоти.

К этому я был не готов. Повторюсь, я представлял все лишь в теории. *Ребенок. Мальчик.* Но не *Личность.* У него были мои губы. Мои волосы. Родимое пятнышко, такое же, как на краю моего правого уха. То ли змея, то ли рыба начала корчиться тогда во мне. Между ребрами. Внутри. Погружаясь все глубже. Ученая протянула ко мне ребенка. Опустила на руки. Страх уронить малыша. Вдруг я его не удержу. Мальчик проснулся, когда я прикоснулся к нему. Его маленькие глазки пытались приспособиться к свету флуоресцентных ламп. Я хотел извиниться перед ним. За то, что первое, что он увидел, не было небом или листвой деревьев. За то, что первое, что он почувствовал, не было ароматным запахом сосен, растущих вдоль тропы возле нашего дома.

Согласно тому, что я читал, я должен был его поцеловать. Это было бы проявлением любви. Я сжал губы. Наклонил шею. Но понял, что не могу.

Затем. Затем малыш сам потянулся ко мне. Его маленькая ручка—связка из мясистых комков. Такая теплая на моих губах. Поцелуй. Он улыбнулся. Как мне казалось, это была улыбка. По крайней мере, это было чем-то знакомым. Подобное я видел на старых пленочных видеозаписях, найденных на бабушкином чердаке. Отец качает меня на руках. Я беззубый. Счастливый. Пленка прыгает, подгорает по краям. Другое чувство посетило меня тогда. Не мечущееся, словно угорь, а нежное, светящееся. «Вы рады?»—спросила женщина. Я кивнул головой и промычал что-то в знак согласия. «Как вы его назовете?»

Я провел дни, мучаясь этим вопросом. Купил книгу имен и их значений. Набрасывал варианты, пока стоял в очереди, во время просмотра фильма и когда просыпался посреди ночи. Я нашел подходящее имя. Сильное. Такое имя было защищено от любых школьных обзывательств. Несмотря на это, я почему-то ответил: «Леопольд».

Если бы я мог изменить этот миг, проглотить слово до того,

как оно просочилось в ее уши, я бы непременно это сделал. Она улыбнулась, посмотрела на мальчика и сказала: «Так и запишем». В этот момент у моего ребенка появилось имя. Если бы я только мог поменять его так просто, как кличку питомцев в детстве. Но имя ребенка, человека—это серьезно. Его имя не подлежало изменению.

Я принес мальчика домой. Мы прошлись по тенистой тропинке вдоль сосен «Вдохни этот запах,—прошептал я,—так пахнет мир». «Чувствуешь, как прохладно в тени?» Его глаза были широко открыты. Все оставляло след в его сознании. Оно было пристанищем всего, что еще появится в его снах, словно тусклое воспоминание, которое он не способен отчетливо понять.

Затем я показал ему дом. Мы побывали в каждой комнате. Смотрели на книги. Арт-объекты, украшающие полки и стены. Я отнес малыша в его комнату. Показал ему выкрашенные стены. Затем я опустил его в кроватку на мягкий матрас, почти такой же крошечный, как он сам. Он начал вертеться. Его ручки. Его ножки. Морское создание в панцире. Умоляет, чтобы его повернули, как он хочет. Я мягко положил руку на его животик. Маленькие толстые ручки ринулись к центру, и он улыбнулся. «Малыш»,—сказал я.

Когда мальчик уснул, я принялся за работу. Округлял числа, делил, слагал, уравнивал. Моей ответственностью были учет доходов и расходов и расчет распределения затрат. Это был мой единственный талант. Составлять отчеты за очень маленький отрезок времени. Другие тратили на это часы и даже дни. В отчетах мир был управляемым. В них не составляло труда устранить возможные неисправности и предвидеть доходы от акций. Ни разу еще я не допустил ошибки в работе. Иногда в моих снах люди превращались в числа. Тогда я выстраивал их в колонки. Вычитал тех, что казались мне потенциальной проблемой. Умножал тех, кто давал мне надежду.

Затем. Затем случилось самое странное. Я пытался вспомнить, о чем были мои сны в детстве, но не мог. Это взволновало меня до такой степени, что я перестал работать. Я поднялся в комнату, где спал малыш и наблюдал за его сном. Я хотел наклониться ближе, как него под веками шевельнулись глазные яблоки. Что ему снилось? Я надеялся, что его сны были о сосновых деревьях, свежем воздухе, обо мне, а не о синтетической околоплодной жидкости, ослепляющем белом свете или ученых. Мне показалось, что на момент ребенок перестал дышать. Меня как током ударило. Как будто почувствовав это, мальчик открыл глаза, повернул головку в сторону и вытянул свои маленькие розовые ручки. Затем он приоткрыл губы, и из этого тельца раздался крик настолько свирепый, что стекла задрожали.

У меня чуть ноги не отказали. Как такое было возможно? Это был первобытный рев.

С тех пор он ни на секунду не сомкнул глаз. Уставился на меня, будто говоря: «Ты, да, ты—источник моей боли». Я взял его на руки, и он дотронулся до моего лица. Улыбнулся. Радостно гукнул. Я отметил про себя, что уход за ребенком был верным занятием.

Ребенок спал лишь время от времени, и я использовал эти

моменты для работы. Когда он просыпался, он кричал. Весь дом сотрясался. Светильники качались на цепях. Я бежал наверх, держал его на руках, ворковал над ним. Он улыбался. Хохотал. Бормотал что-то на доступном только ему языке. Я садился в удобное кресло и покачивал его на руках, солнце грело нас. Порой я мог задремать. Ребенок тогда пытался меня укусить. Сжимал челюстенки. Но у него получалось только посасывать мою кожу. Иногда это будило меня, а в те моменты, когда это не срабатывало, он вопил и лупил меня, пока миссия не была выполнена.

—

Он спал редко, что скоро сказалось на моем состоянии. Я засыпал пока подогревал смесь. Мог задремать на унитазе. Рухнуть на пол, завязывая шнурки.

Я начал брать малыша с собой в кровать. Мы лежали в темноте, и я обвивал его руками, чтобы он не чувствовал себя брошенным. Это сработало на какое-то время, но с процессом его роста, требования его также увеличивались. Само мое нахождение рядом было уже недостаточным. Он хотел, чтобы я говорил с ним, поэтому я записал свой голос и поставил на повтор. Но он начал распознавать повторяющиеся обороты моей речи. Тогда я записал несколько разных предложений и включил случайное воспроизведение, чтобы мальчику было сложнее предугадать их последовательность. Это дало мне пару свободных часов в течение нескольких дней.

IV.

Мальчик развивался с изумительной скоростью. Он пытался говорить и, наверное, я должен был гордиться этим, но каждое его слово, было немного неверным. Он, например, говорил «желый» вместо «желтый»; «шать-шать» вместо «кушать»; «малюбка» вместо «малютка». Но ничто так не смущало меня, как «бапа». Каждая ошибка напоминала мне о его искусственности. Капля моей ДНК, малая толика, булавочный укол. Ребенок набирал вес с тревожной скоростью. Он был уже вдвое больше обычного младенца. Приземистые конечности были все еще не в состоянии нести на себе массу его тела. А чтобы начать ползать ему не хватало решимости.

Аппетит мальчика продолжал расти. Иногда за день он мог съесть целую коробку детского питания. Голод его становился сильнее, и молоко перестало ему нравится, он отказался от бутылочки, и я пытался кормить его с ложечки. С края тарелки. С рук. Я пытался найти решение в книгах о воспитании детей. В одной из них предлагалось использовать накладную грудь. Я ходил по дому враскорячку, обмотанный этим приспособлением, а ребенок лишь смотрел на меня, его рот открывался и закрывался, как если бы он был окунем, глотающим воздух. И все же есть он не мог.

Затем. Затем он начал издавать новый шум. Казалось, словно нежную ткань его горла, сырую, розовую, кто-то резал. Это продолжалось несколько дней. Я перепробовал различное детское питание, овощи, фрукты, конфеты, в конце концов. Ничто не было угодно малышу.

Сначала я хотел перестать есть из солидарности, но чувствовал дрожь, качая ребенка на руках. «Малыш,—сказал я ему,—малыш, пожалуйста, я так слаб. Я так устал». «Шать-шать»,—орал он тогда, врезая шипы своего крика мне в голову.

Мне нужна была помощь, но обратиться было толком не к кому. Я переехал в сюда с моей тогда-еще-женой, иногда общался с коллегами по работе. Отношения с друзьями детства сошли на нет. Остались только я и мальчик.

И как-то так вышло, что я решил попросить помощи у бывшей.

Мой звонок однозначно поставил ее в замешательство. «Пожалуйста,—умолял я ее,—я не знаю как быть».

—

Я взял ребенка на руки. Покачал его. Прошептал ему что-то вроде того, что в книгах советуют шептать малышам. Он наконец-то заснул. Стекла перестали дрожать. Я медленно опустился на диван. Руки ослабли от его тяжести. Мне снилось, как мальчик разрушает город. Топчет крыши домов своими коренастыми ножками. Опрокидывает водонапорные башни, рекламные щиты, телефонные столбы. В одном из зданий я увидел женщину, она звала меня. Ребенок почти ее раздавил, но я проснулся. Рядом стояла моя бывшая жена. Она звала меня по имени.

Она сразу же обратила внимание на габариты мальчика. Сказала: «Боже мой». Сказала: «Какой огромный». Сказала: «Размером с дом». Спросила: «С ним что-то не так?» Я сказал: «Да. Он ничего не ест». Она обхватила его талию. Попыталась взять на руки. Мальчик тревожно встрепенулся. Его глаза широкие от недоверия. Глядя на меня, он изобразил что-то вроде усмешки. Как мне показалось. Расслабился. Позволил, чтобы его взяли на руки. Она начала качать мальчика на руках. Он, спокойный поначалу, взял и укусил ее. Моя бывшая жена отдернула руку. Посмотрела на него так, будто он ее предал. На руке остались слюни. «Слава богу у него нет зубов»,— сказала она.

Затем. Затем ребенок заорал. Непривыкшая к шуму, моя бывшая жена подпрыгнула, и мальчик выскользнул у нее из рук и упал на пол. «Ай»,—он кричал. «Бапа»,—он звал. Он завопил, и окна снова задрожали. Моя бывшая жена закрыла уши. Посмотрела на меня с таким лицом, которого я за годы совместной жизни не видел ни разу. Думаю, я должен был прийти в ярость. Накричать на нее за то, что она уронила мальчика. Но я не сделал этого. Может, потому что был очень слаб от голода и недостатка сна. Я взял ребенка на руки, но это не усмирило его беспокойства.

Моя бывшая жена отступила назад. В сторону кухни. Ее руки застыли в воздухе. Она оторвала несколько бумажных полотенец и скрутила из них нечто вроде берушей. Покачала головой и вытащила из холодильника говяжий фарш. Слепила котлеты, по форме напоминавшие маленькие луны. Налила масла на сковородку и начала жарить котлеты. В один момент она пристально посмотрела в окно. Сказала: «Боже мой. Терпеть не могу взгляд койотов».

Они царапали заднюю дверь. Их миски были пустыми. «Я не покормил их сегодня»,—сказал я. Один из них заскулил. Мальчик взглянул на меня. На его красном личике образовалась улыбка. Я издал небольшой вой. Мальчик повторил за мной. Койоты снова завыли. Мальчик повторил за ними. «Они уходят,—сказала моя бывшая жена.—Думаешь они вернутся?» «Нет,—ответил я,—вряд ли».

Моя бывшая жена вытащила котлеты со сковороды и принесла их нам. Целая солнечная система на тарелке. Сначала она дала одну мне. Промолвила: «Не стоит кормить младенцев мясом, но, может, чуть-чуть не навредит». Я собрался положить кусок в рот, но мальчик выхватил его. Запихал лунный шарик прямо в розовую беззубую пещеру своего рта. Разжевал, как мог, и проглотил. Когда моя бывшая жена попыталась дать ему еще, он в ужасе отпрянул. Она сказала: «Ох, малыш»,—и наклонилась к нему снова. Он прильнул ко мне, зарываясь головой в подмышку. Вдруг он зарычал и устремился вперед. Принялся кусать ее за палец. Так до самой кисти. Головой болтает. Рыба на крючке.

Она уронила тарелку. Мясо упало на пол. Упорядоченные планеты, покатились под диван. Ребенок завопил. Его ручки потянулись в сторону мясных сфер, разбросанных у моих ног. Моя бывшая жена собрала их. «Нет,— сказала она,— мы не едим с пола». Малыш закричал. Он плевался и шипел. Он был силен. Гораздо сильнее, чем обычный ребенок.

—

Моя бывшая жена направилась в сторону кухни. Выбросила котлеты в мусорку. Сказала, что я сам разберусь. Что ребенок так же несносен, как я. Она выглянула в окно и ушла.

Я достал котлеты из мусорной корзины. Дал немного мальчику и немного поел сам. Слегка набравшись сил, я вытащил оставшийся фарш из холодильника. Посадил мальчика на стол. Начал лепить шарики из холодной розоватой массы. Мальчик схватил кусок сырого фарша. Я попытался вырвать мясо из его рук, но было слишком поздно. Фарша и след простыл. Мальчик улыбнулся, потянулся за добавкой. «Нет»,—сказал я. И снова крик. Загрохотали столовые приборы в ящиках. Крышки кастрюль. Ключи на крючках.

Мальчику было невозможно угодить. Его аппетиты росли наряду с неугомонностью. Он не оставлял меня в покое ни на минуту. Я закрыл глаза. Заткнул уши. Пел ему. Качал на руках. А он все продолжал что-то лепетать. Издавать слюняво пузырящийся шум. Подпевать завыванию койотов по ночам. Он стал неумолкаем.

Разница между днем и ночью становилась все незаметнее, пока совсем не исчезла. Дни превратились в череду шума и ерзания. Я потерял способность работать. Не мог удержать в голове ни одну мысль.

Я позвонил в лабораторию. Спросил, было ли хоть что-то из этого нормальным. Попросил о помощи. Хоть какой-то. «Им нужны физические упражнения»,—ответила ученая. «Отвезите ребенка на природу. Таким детям нужна стимуляция. Они отличаются от обычных детей,—сказала она.—Вы должны научить его находить связь между действием и последствием». «Что мне для этого сделать?»—спросил я. «Возьмите его на прогулку в парк»,—сказала она.

День постепенно подходил к концу. Солнце приближалось к горизонту. Я встал, взял со стола ключи. Упаковал несколько ломтиков нарезанного мяса с собой в дорогу. Взял на руки мальчика—он тем временем всячески извивался, пытаясь дотянуться до сумки с сырым мясом. «Не сейчас»,—сказал я. Он издал короткий рык. Показал свои влажные десны. Мы подошли к машине; я посадил его пухлое тельце на крышу. Одной рукой я придерживал его, а другой вытащил мясо. «Вот, держи»,—промолвил я. Он схватил кусок. Вакуум рта втянул мясо целиком.

Пристегнуть мальчика в автокресле не составило труда. Он похлопал себя по животу. Облизал руки. Пропел какую-то детскую тарабарщину. Гудел и пускал слюни. Попытался дотронуться до меня. Погладить по лицу. «Бапа»,—сказал он. Я отодвинулся назад. Сказал: «Я хочу показать тебе, как течет река меж берегов. Как сосны растут на холмах». Мальчик захлопал. Сказал: «Зосы».

Мы проехали город. Спустились в долину. Солнце мерцало на коже ребенка. Его лицо полыхало. Впитывало все вокруг, каждый проносящийся мимо пейзаж. Мальчик взглянул на меня через зеркало заднего вида. Улыбнулся. Когда мы проезжали под железным переплетением решетчатого моста, рот его вылепил форму чудесного полумесяца. В глазах отражались затейливые треугольники.

—

Щелчок, ремень безопасности отстегнут, и мальчик у меня на руках. Я пронес его вдоль тропинки, сплошь устеленной словно заржавевшими сосновыми иголками. В прохладной тени жизнь замедлила бег. Запах пьянил. «Зосы»,—сказал мальчик. Он только и успевал вертеть головой. «Да»,—ответил я. Вдали наконец показалась река. Мы лавировали между деревьями. Я нашел укромную поляну, на которую еще проникала последняя полоса вечернего света. Теплая и приятная. Я уложил мальчика в сосновую колыбель.

Он засмеялся. Сделал ноги лягушкой. Пятки касались друг друга. Он схватил горсть сосновых иголок. Подкинул их. Хихикал, когда они сыпались на него. Он проделал так несколько раз, пуская пузыри изо рта и фыркая. Я отошел назад. Медленно, шаг за шагом. Еще шаг. Глубже в лесную чащу. Еще шаг. К чернильным стволам деревьев. «Бапа»,— сказал мальчик. Он больше не подбрасывал иголки. Я мог уйти. Уйти и не вернуться. Выспаться. Наконец-то выспаться. Я повернулся. Направился к машине. Ночь сгущалась над мальчиком. Он звал меня. Я дошел до двери. Остановился. Взялся за ручку. Но не смог. Не смог оставить ребенка.

V.

Когда у мальчика начали прорезаться зубы, я был почти полностью погружен в сон. Его нужды сильно утомили меня. Тело сдавало позиции. Я больше не мог держать глаза открытыми. И в этом потоке почти полного сна я почувствовал острую боль. Сгусток белого света в районе руки. Я открыл глаза. Увидел его десны. Губы, расплывшиеся в ухмылке. Острым краем зуба он почти прокусил мою кожу. Как же быстро прорезался первый зуб. Нежная розовая ткань набухла вокруг него. Я высвободил руку. Поднялся с постели. Взял мальчика с собой вниз. Дал ему немного мяса.

В тот день я решил, что мы пойдем есть на улицу. Раз уж мальчику хочется мяса, я приготовлю его на гриле. Добавлю овощей. Мальчик подышит свежим воздухом, пока не стало слишком прохладно. Пока ветки сосен не опустились под тяжестью снега. А небо не стало низким.

Он был слишком большим для своего высокого стула. Широкие, длинные ноги. Задница плотно умещалась в сиденье. Он мог дотянуться до подноса и дотронуться до края стола.

Я разжег гриль. С тех пор как моя бывшая жена ушла, я едва прикасался к нему. Сама мысль об этом была мучительна. Я вспоминал вечера, которые мы проводили сидя за этим столом с подвыпившими коллегами. Дым от мяса клубился на деревьях. «Начнем все с чистого листа»,—сказал я мальчику, смешивая нарезанные овощи—морковь, горох, кукурузу. Я высыпал их в большую металлической посудину и добавил говядину. Отличное получилось месиво. Скатал шарики. Сплюснул каждый, придав им форму дисков. Мальчик был взволнован, глядя на языки пламени. Вслушиваясь в шипение мяса.

Пока я копался с грилем, ребенок не находил себе места от голода. Начал хлопать руками по столику. Пластмассовый поднос дребезжал. Неожиданно он замер. Глаза мальчика наполнились любопытством.

На низкой ветке возле него стрекотала белка. «Белка»,— сказал я. Мальчик взглянул на меня, затем на белку. «Бека»,— сказал он. «Да,—сказал я,—белка». Я отломил кусочек хлеба. Положил на тропинку, которая вела от ветки к его столику, чтобы мальчик мог получше разглядеть зверька.

Я следил за мясом. Переворачивал котлеты каждые несколько

минут. Думал о белках, которые цокали по утрам. Как моя бывшая жена ненавидела их. Говорила, что от них можно ждать любой пакости. Называла их коричневыми крысами. Но мне они всегда нравились. Я восхищался их умением прыгать с веток на провода. Взбираться по кирпичным стенам и запасаться орехами и ягодами. Прирожденные счетоводы. Продуманные и экономные. Готовятся к периоду, когда студенты больше не будут подкармливать их. Поставка хлеба и конфет прекратится.

Я положил бургер на тарелку перед мальчиком. Он сразу смахнул с котлеты булочку. Понюхал мясной диск. Нахмурился. Посмотрел на меня, затем на белку, которая тем временем настороженно спустилась на тропинку. Мальчик улыбнулся. Вытянул ручки. Они напоминали щупальца в воздухе. «Прошу тебя»,—сказал я, еле держась на ногах от усталости. «Пожалуйста, съешь котлету». Мальчик даже бровью не повел. Я решил приготовить котлету без овощей. Надавив на нее лопаточкой, выжал кровавый сок. Тот шипел и дымился.

Эту котлету ребенок тоже есть не стал, отправив ее прямиком на землю. Пока белка не успела ее перехватить, это сделал я. Положил котлету на стол к предыдущей, отвергнутой. Я подошел к грилю, чтобы приготовить нечто более сырое. В голову закрался шепот, заставший меня врасплох. Стало быть, мальчик жаждал ощутить вкус крови? С этой мыслью пришло чувство расшатанности. В нем я завис. Жар, исходивший от гриля, действовал усыпляюще. Я был где-то между сном и реальностью. «Как долго,—думал я,—человек может обойтись без сна?»

Отдаленный визг белки перемешался с потоком моих мыслей. Звук царапания когтей по деревянным ножкам стола. Грохот тарелок. Веселый хохот мальчика. Пронзительный вопль прошел сквозь меня. Мою спину, мышцы, нервные окончания, спинномозговую жидкость. Все тело пульсировало и дрожало. Я вернулся к реальности и обернулся. Лопаточка вылетела у меня из рук. С грохотом упала на землю.

—

Белка была у мальчика в руках. Он рвал и драл ее внутренности так, что кусочки жилистой плоти оставались на его подбородке. С сосредоточенным выражением лица он вцепился в живот зверька своим единственным резцом. Мех и кишки стекали по подбородку вдоль шеи вместе с экскрементами и мочой.

Я ринулся спасать белку из захвата мальчика, стульчик упал. Белка приземлилась в метре от него. Ленты внутренностей струились следом.

Мальчик заорал. Его огромное тело в отчаянии пыталось ползти, что давалось ему сложно. Я перешагнул через него. Пусть кричит. Плачет. Сжимает и разжимает кулаки. Белый свет солнца сердито опустился на его тело. Я смотрел на белку, ее маленькое тельце дрожало, пыталось ползти. Глаза зверька почти закрылись, оставив лишь тонкие прорези. Когда они открылись, это были уже два черных зеркала. В их отражении я увидел свою ногу. Она увеличивалась. А когда достигла головы зверька, его задние лапки дернулись в последней попытке сбежать. Затем. Затем я раздавил белку. Это была единственно возможная пощада.

Ребенок был у меня на руках. Он был возмущен. «Плохой бапа»—сказал он. «Мое»,—сказал он. «Мое-мое». Я положил его на кухонную столешницу. Обработал раны. Пероксид водорода шипел, добравшись до царапин. Фосфоресцировал на кусочках кожи по краям. Он не плакал. Он хотел белку. «Мое-мое-мое-мое!» Когда же моего ответа не последовало, он прикусил мою руку. Я попытался высвободить ее, но он вдавил резец между костяшками. Кровь медленно наводнила края губ мальчика. Я был вне себя от злости. Но мальчик лишь сильнее вцепился в руку. «Я принесу белку»,—закричал я, и он разжал челюсти. Рот его вылепил кровавую улыбку, и мальчик захлопал своими ужасными маленькими ручками.

Я поднял останки животного с земли. Отнес их на кухню. Дал их ему в руки. Прислонился к стене и съехал по ней на кафельный пол. Когда я обернул бинтом рану от укуса, с нее еще сочилась кровь. Комната превратилась в вихрь шума. Гул холодильника, чавканье пирующего мальчика. Я закрыл глаза и представил, как он охотится на животных. Сжирает их. Дом пропитан запахом гнили. Мальчик идет в подготовительную группу. Кусает детей. Сжирает их.

Какое-то время я провел в беспамятстве. Провалился в бездну сна, но проснулся, услышав голос ребенка. Грохот стекла. Дребезжание кастрюль и сковородок. Пинки толстых ножек. Он съел почти все без остатка. Отделил плоть и шерсть от костей с невероятной точностью. Навык, полученный по наследству. Спящий ген. Окровавленные кости лежали на столешнице в определенном порядке. Выстроенная схема его обеда.

Солнце уже село. Ночь притихла, был слышен только вой койотов и гул насекомых. Мальчик потянулся ко мне. Указал на остатки его пищи. И на свой живот. «Мое»,—сказал он. «Грр»,—огрызнулся он. Затем. Затем он резко замолк. Повернул голову на зов койотов. Засмеялся и издал похожий вопль.

—

Голова моя, несмотря на краткий сон, была неподвижна. Мне становилось хуже. Усталость лежала на голове как тяжелая мокрая тряпка. Веки почти закрылись. Я оставил заднюю дверь открытой, дошел до гаража и вытащил собачий корм. Я начал наполнять им миски, но быстро остановился и направился обратно к дому. По пути я разбрасывал кусочки корма так, чтобы получилась тропинка. От тротуара вверх по лестнице. Через дверной проход. Ведущий к мальчику. Я остановился. Снял мальчика со столешницы. Положил его на пол. Его пухлые конечности извивались на кафельном полу. Я достал пакеты с замороженным мясом из холодильника. Положил куски мяса на пол— ужин для мальчика.

Когда он схватил кусок, я отошел назад.

«Бапа»,—кричал он, рот его полон мяса.

Затем. Затем я отвернулся.

И больше уже не поворачивался.

«Бапа»,—крикнул он, громче на этот раз. Извиваясь. Пытаясь ползти за мной. «Бапа?»

Я услышал визг койотов на улице. Закрыл глаза.

«Бапа?»

Не промолвив ни слова, я закрыл дверь между кухней и залом. Поднялся вверх по лестнице. Закрывая каждую дверь между ним и мной. Я опустился на кровать. В темноту. Где меня быстро настиг прилив сна. Мое тело плавало между сном и реальностью. Я почти не слышал визга собравшихся койотов. Помню только, как сказал: «Ешьте».

———

На следующий день я проснулся с ощущением чего-то нового. Тело было будто наэлектризованным от одной мысли о слове «ешьте». Наверное оно просочилось в мой сон. Каждый раз звучало все громче предыдущего. Пока не стало совсем слепящим и шипящим. Сон дал мне сил, но встать все равно было сложно. Я мог передвигаться только очень медленно. С остановками. Вниз по лестнице. Открывая каждую дверь. До тех пор, пока я не очутился возле двери, ведущей на кухню.

Когда я открыл дверь, я увидел койота. Его холодное тело лежало на полу. Глотка вырвана. Спутанные внутренности торчали с боков. Кровавые следы от лап были еще сырые. Стены в царапинах. Эпицентр красных широких мазков жестокости находился там, где я оставил мальчика. Я прошелся по тропинке во дворе. Не нашел ни одного его следа. Я обошел дом. Обыскал все по пути, которому следовали обычно койоты, когда возвращались в лес. На речной отмели я остановился. Тело найдено не было. Новое колющее чувство возникло тогда во мне. С одной стороны, будто якорь повис, с другой—буй.

Я вернулся домой. Навел порядок. Снял кормушки с деревьев. Попытался вернуться к привычной жизни. К числам. Ко сну. И попытка удалась. На какое-то время. Я избегал звонков бывшей жены. Удалял с автоответчика сообщения, в которых она спрашивала о здоровье мальчика.

Жизнь снова становилась нормальной. Тихой. Упорядоченной. Затем. Затем я увидел ту новостную передачу. Услышал, как ведущие смеются. Как удивляются бреду, который якобы выдумывают люди. Я сидел на диване. Я наколол на вилку кусок тофу и поднес ко рту, но остановился, когда почувствовал что-то в районе спины. В одной из частей позвоночника, которая никак не волновала меня до этого момента. Где мышечные ткани срастаются. Плотно упаковывают тела позвонков. И распадаются на малейшие частицы.

Я вошел в комнату, где стоял отцовский оружейный шкаф. Достал ружье. Гладкая древесина. Вес его пугающий. Не уверенный в том, испортились ли патроны, я все-таки зарядил несколько. Взвел курок. Смог бы я сделать это? Пристрелить мальчика? Весь день я провел, то держа ружье в руках, то опуская его. Пытаясь сделать выбор. В конце концов, я вернул его обратно в сейф. Сел на диван в зале. Наблюдал, как солнце утекает из дома. Сумерки заполняли каждый его уголок, медленно ложились на кухонную плитку. На то место, где мальчик расправился с койотом. Где койоты сделали то, что они в итоге сделали с мальчиком. Я сидел там и ждал. Каждый вечер я ждал, когда мой мальчик вернется.

Acknowledgements

I would like to thank Caleb Michael Sarvis for putting such great care in publishing this book with Bridge Eight Press. I would also like to thank Brian Evenson, Eric LaRocca, and Julia Liz Elliott for their generosity in preparing quotes for the jacket of this book. I would like to thank my wife, Alisa, for her support and careful eye on my work. She is a wonder. I am grateful for the many editors who published these stories in their earlier forms. Journals and small presses are the lifesblood of the writing world. I'd also like to thank the following people for their support over the years: Robert Pennington, Andy Tinsley, Vincent Comparetto, The Notlemeyer family, Ben Hagen, McCormick Templeman, Jeremy Jackson, and Nicole Suazo. Also, my sister who does not understand my work, but supports me nonetheless. Finally, my brother who passed away this holiday season after his painful battle with cancer.